Falling Shadows: Vanishing Truths, Deadly Pursuits, & Darkness Within

FALLING SHADOWS

First edition. April 4, 2025.

ISBN: 978-9349569959

Written by Nya Luther King.

Also by Nya Luther King

Global Affair
A Global Affair

Ironheart Academy
Ironheart Academy: The Forbidden Library Hidden Secrets

Psychologist
Shadows in Silicon Valley
Shattered Reflections
Falling Shadows

Shadows of Power
Shadows of Power

The AI Uprising
The AI Uprising
AI Uprising II: The Overmind

AI vs. The Digital Empire
AI x Human Code

The Catalyst Code
The Catalyst Code

Standalone
The Final Witness
Chasing Shadows
The Dark Descent

Watch for more at Thrillmind.com.

Table of Contents

To those who chase the light through the falling shadows of their own hearts—this story is yours.

To my loved ones, who stood by me as I navigated the darkness within these pages, and to the readers brave enough to unravel the vanishing truths: may you find strength in the pursuit, even when the shadows deepen.

With gratitude and shadows,

Nya Luther King

"In the shadow of every truth lies a darkness waiting to consume it."— Dr.Raam Harvard

"Love is a shadow—chase it, and it flees; turn away, and it follows, deadly."— Dr.Raam Harvard

"We are all shadows, cast by the light of our own lies."— Friedrich Nietzsche

Chapter 1: Introducing Dr. Sam Cross

Dr. Sam Cross leaned against the polished mahogany desk in his bright, airy office, the warm afternoon light filtering through the large windows. His gaze drifted over the scattered papers and books lining the shelves, a mix of psychological texts, personal journals, and the latest bestsellers. Each item told a story, yet none compared to the narrative that played out in the lives of his patients.

A framed certificate hung prominently on the wall, proclaiming his accolades in psychology. Sam had built a reputation as one of the leading psychologists in Silicon Valley, specializing in trauma recovery and mental health resilience. His office was a haven for those seeking refuge from their emotional struggles—a safe space where vulnerability was met with understanding and compassion.

The soft chime of the clock on the wall signaled the arrival of his next appointment, jolting him from his reverie. He adjusted his glasses and took a deep breath, shaking off the remnants of distraction. Today was particularly special; he had a new patient, and Sam always approached new beginnings with a mix of excitement and trepidation.

As the door opened, a young woman stepped inside, her presence electric yet fragile. Lena Hart, a software developer, seemed to carry the weight of the world on her slender shoulders. Sam rose to greet her, his professional demeanor instantly shifting to one of warmth.

"Lena, it's a pleasure to meet you. Please, have a seat," he said, gesturing to the comfortable chair opposite his desk.

"Thanks, Dr. Cross," she replied, her voice barely above a whisper as she sank into the chair, her eyes flitting around the room, absorbing the safe environment.

Sam settled back into his own chair, his curiosity piqued. "What brings you here today?"

Lena hesitated, her fingers twisting in her lap. "I've been struggling with... a lot of things," she finally admitted, her voice trembling. "I thought talking to someone might help."

Sam nodded, his expression empathetic. "That's a great first step. I want you to know that this is a safe space. You can share whatever you feel comfortable with."

As they began to talk, Sam listened intently, absorbing her words and emotions like a sponge. Lena spoke of the pressures of her job in the fast-paced tech industry, the demands of creating groundbreaking software, and the toxic environment that often left her feeling isolated. Sam recognized the patterns of stress and trauma woven into her narrative, and he sensed the deeper layers of her experience—things she wasn't ready to reveal yet.

As the session progressed, Sam's mind raced with possibilities. He recognized the signs of past trauma lurking beneath the surface, waiting to be unearthed. He wanted to guide her through this, to help her confront the shadows that haunted her.

When the hour ended, Lena left the office, a flicker of hope ignited in her eyes. Sam watched her go, a familiar feeling washing over him—a blend of professional satisfaction and personal longing. Helping others heal was his passion, but there was something about Lena that struck a deeper chord within him.

The Next Day

The following day, as Sam prepared for another session, he found himself reflecting on his own life. Despite his success, he often felt an emptiness that echoed in his heart. He had dedicated himself to his patients, pouring his energy into their healing, yet he rarely allowed himself to be vulnerable. The irony wasn't lost on him; he was a psychologist who understood trauma and connection, yet he struggled to form genuine bonds outside his practice.

His thoughts were interrupted by a knock on the door. It was Dr. Maya Chen, his colleague and trusted friend. She stepped in, her presence bringing a sense of comfort.

"Hey, Sam! Ready for another day of saving the world?" she teased, a playful smile on her face.

"Just trying to help a few people along the way," he replied, returning her smile.

Maya's demeanor shifted, her expression growing serious. "You seem a bit off today. Everything okay?"

Sam sighed, leaning back in his chair. "I had a new patient yesterday—Lena Hart. She's brilliant, but I can sense there's something deeper she's not ready to share."

Maya nodded knowingly. "You have a knack for seeing past the surface. It's both your strength and your curse."

"True," Sam said, rubbing the bridge of his nose. "But I can't help but feel that she's hiding something significant. I want to help her, but it's challenging when they don't open up."

"Just give her time," Maya reassured him. "You know how this works. Trust builds gradually."

They shared a laugh, but as Maya left the room, Sam couldn't shake the feeling that Lena's story was more intertwined with his own than he realized. The world of Silicon Valley was rife with ambition, but beneath the glitzy surface lay shadows that often went unspoken.

The Gala Invitation

Days passed, and Sam continued to see Lena weekly. Each session brought a little more light to her darkness, but she remained guarded, unwilling to fully delve into the shadows of her past. Just when he thought they were making progress, a new complication arose.

An invitation arrived for a high-profile gala celebrating innovation in technology, hosted by one of the biggest firms in Silicon Valley. The event was known for attracting the elite, from entrepreneurs to investors, all eager to showcase their achievements. Sam had attended similar events before, but this time, he felt an inexplicable pull to go.

He found himself pacing in his office, the invitation crumpled in his hand. Should he go? Was this just another superficial gathering, or could it lead to something significant—perhaps even a chance to connect with Lena outside the confines of the therapy room?

That evening, after a long day of sessions, Sam decided to take a leap of faith. He put on his best suit, polished his shoes, and prepared to step into a world of glamour. Maybe he could reach Lena in a way he hadn't been able to during their sessions. Maybe, just maybe, this gala would unveil the hidden connections between their lives.

The Gala Night

As he entered the grand ballroom, Sam was overwhelmed by the opulence surrounding him. Crystal chandeliers sparkled above, casting a warm glow over the crowd dressed in elegant attire. He navigated through the sea of people, exchanging pleasantries with familiar faces while scanning the room for Lena.

Finally, he spotted her—an ethereal vision in a shimmering gown that hugged her figure in all the right places. Her laughter danced through the air as she chatted animatedly with a group of tech executives, her confidence shining through the crowd. But as he approached, he noticed a flicker of apprehension in her eyes when she caught sight of him.

"Dr. Cross!" she exclaimed, her smile faltering slightly. "What a surprise!"

"Lena, you look stunning," he said, his heart racing. "I didn't know you would be here."

"Just trying to make connections," she replied, her voice light but her eyes betraying deeper emotions.

They moved to a quieter corner, their conversation flowing more freely than it had in the office. As they talked about the industry and their shared passion for mental health, Sam felt the walls between them beginning to dissolve. The energy shifted; the air crackled with an unspoken tension that left them both breathless.

But just as Sam was about to delve deeper, the atmosphere shifted once more—a sudden commotion erupted at the other end of the ballroom, a deafening noise that shattered their moment. Sam's instincts kicked in; he sensed that something was terribly wrong.

The Shift

As the crowd gasped and murmured in confusion, Lena's expression turned pale. Sam's heart raced; he could feel the dread building within him. Before he could react, Lena's gaze flicked to the chaos, and in a heartbeat, she was gone, swallowed by the throng of guests scrambling for the exits.

Panic surged through him. The connection they had just begun to forge was suddenly threatened by something far more sinister. Sam moved swiftly, weaving through the crowd, desperation propelling him forward. What had just happened? Why did it feel as if a shadow had fallen over the entire evening?

And as he pushed through the throng, he couldn't shake the feeling that this gala was more than just an event; it was the catalyst that would set into motion a series of events that would change everything for him and Lena.

DR. SAM CROSS WAS NO longer just a psychologist dedicated to helping others; he was a man drawn into a web of intrigue, mystery, and danger. With Lena now at the center of it all, he was determined to uncover the truth—not just for her sake, but for his own as well. The path ahead was uncertain, but Sam knew he had to embrace it, for their connection and the shadows that haunted them were just beginning to reveal their secrets.

Chapter 2: Silicon Valley gala

The opulence of the gala enveloped Dr. Sam Cross as he stepped further into the grand ballroom, a vast space adorned with golden chandeliers and glimmering decor that reflected the affluence of Silicon Valley's elite. The hum of conversation mixed with the soft strains of a live orchestra, creating an atmosphere of anticipation and excitement. For most, this was a night to showcase achievements and network; for Sam, it was an opportunity to connect with Lena beyond the confines of his office.

As he adjusted his tie and surveyed the crowd, a mix of curiosity and anxiety churned in his stomach. He had never been one for lavish events, preferring the quiet introspection of his office and the solace of his work. Yet tonight felt different. He was drawn to the idea of discovering more about Lena Hart—the enigmatic woman who had opened up a new world of possibilities for him, both personally and professionally.

Sam's mind drifted back to their last session. Lena had spoken of her struggles with self-doubt, the pressure of working in a cutthroat environment, and the shadows of her past that lingered just below the surface. He remembered the vulnerability in her voice and the flicker of pain in her eyes as she recounted the moments that had shaped her life. It was this sincerity that had ignited a desire within him to help her not just as a psychologist, but as someone who genuinely cared.

Searching for Lena

Navigating through the throng of guests, Sam smiled politely at familiar faces, exchanging pleasantries while keeping an eye out for Lena. She had mentioned she would attend, but there were no guarantees in this world of high expectations and unexpected absences. As he made his way to the bar for a drink, he overheard snippets of conversations about groundbreaking apps, funding rounds, and tech startups—the usual chatter of a Silicon Valley gala.

He glanced around, spotting a few notable figures in the crowd—investors, CEOs, and innovators who had transformed the tech landscape. Yet none of them held his attention like Lena. As he took a sip of his drink, his mind wandered back to her—how her expressive eyes had shone with intelligence and vulnerability during their sessions, a captivating combination that left him intrigued and wanting more.

"Dr. Cross!" A voice broke through his reverie. He turned to see Maya Chen approaching, her vibrant personality radiating as she greeted him with a warm smile.

"Hey, Maya! Good to see you here," Sam replied, genuinely pleased. "You look fantastic."

"Thanks! Just trying to fit in among all these tech moguls," she said, her eyes scanning the room. "Are you here for any specific reason, or just enjoying the free champagne?"

"A bit of both, I suppose," he replied, the truth about his interest in Lena lingering just below the surface.

Maya raised an eyebrow knowingly. "Still not taking the plunge into the social scene? I thought maybe you'd want to network a bit."

"I'm not here for business," Sam said, his tone more serious. "I'm actually hoping to run into a new patient of mine—Lena Hart."

Maya's expression shifted to one of understanding. "Ah, Lena! I've heard good things about her. I think she's over by the stage."

Sam's heart raced. "Thanks, Maya. I'll go find her."

The Encounter

With renewed determination, Sam made his way towards the stage, the music growing louder as he approached the crowd gathered near the performers. And then, just as he caught sight of her, his breath hitched in his throat. Lena stood with a small group of colleagues, her beauty accentuated by the soft glow of the chandeliers overhead. She wore a stunning emerald-green dress that clung to her curves and shimmered like a jewel against her pale skin.

Lena's laughter rang out, a melodic sound that drew him closer. As he stepped into her line of sight, their eyes locked. A rush of warmth flooded through him, and he felt a magnetic pull—a connection that transcended their professional relationship.

"Lena!" he called, pushing through the crowd, his heart racing with excitement and nervousness.

"Dr. Cross!" she exclaimed, her eyes lighting up as he approached. "I didn't expect to see you here!"

"Neither did I, but I'm glad I did," he said, his voice steady despite the fluttering in his chest. "You look amazing."

"Thank you! This is a bit overwhelming, isn't it?" She glanced around, taking in the bustling atmosphere.

"It definitely has its own energy," Sam replied, leaning in slightly to hear her better over the music. "How are you finding it so far?"

"It's a lot," she admitted, her eyes reflecting a mix of excitement and apprehension. "I'm here to network, but honestly, I feel out of place."

"Trust me, you're not alone," he said, a reassuring smile playing on his lips. "I feel like I'm stumbling through a maze of egos and ambition."

Lena chuckled softly, and Sam couldn't help but feel a rush of warmth at the sound. Their conversation flowed naturally, as if they had known each other for years rather than just a few sessions. They discussed the event, the tech industry, and their shared experiences in navigating a world filled with high stakes and intense pressure.

A Connection Deepens

As the night wore on, Sam and Lena found themselves drifting toward the balcony, where the cool night air offered a respite from the crowded ballroom. The stars twinkled above, and the distant sound of waves crashing against the shore added a romantic backdrop to their conversation.

"I love how beautiful it is out here," Lena said, leaning against the railing. "It's nice to escape the chaos for a moment."

"It really is," Sam replied, glancing at her with admiration. "I've always found peace in nature, even amidst the chaos of my work."

Lena turned to him, her expression serious. "Do you ever feel like we're living in a world where everything is just for show? Like we're all pretending to be something we're not?"

Her question resonated with him deeply. Sam contemplated her words, recognizing the truth in them. "Absolutely. I think many people wear masks to hide their vulnerabilities. It's easier that way, but it's also incredibly isolating."

Lena nodded, her gaze dropping to the ground. "I've spent so much time trying to fit in, trying to prove myself in this industry. It's exhausting."

"You don't have to prove anything to anyone," Sam said gently. "You're talented and intelligent. Your worth isn't defined by how others see you."

Her eyes met his, and for a moment, the world around them faded. There was a vulnerability in her expression, a yearning for understanding that tugged at Sam's heart. In that instant, he felt a deep connection—a bond formed not just from their roles as psychologist and patient, but as two people navigating the complexities of life.

The Chaos Returns

Just as the moment intensified, a loud crash erupted from inside the gala. Guests gasped and began to scatter, the music abruptly stopping. Sam and Lena exchanged worried glances, instinctively moving back toward the entrance to see what had happened.

The chaos inside was palpable. Security personnel rushed past them, trying to contain the crowd. Sam's instincts kicked in; he needed to protect Lena. He took her hand, leading her away from the commotion.

"Let's find a way out!" he urged, navigating through the panicked guests.

They moved towards a side exit, adrenaline coursing through their veins. Just as they reached the door, a group of people surged forward, and in the chaos, a figure stumbled out, visibly shaken.

"Run! There's been a shooting!" someone shouted, and panic erupted anew.

Sam's heart raced. He turned to Lena, fear etched on his face. "We need to get to safety. Now!"

A Dangerous Escape

As they bolted outside, the cool night air hit them like a splash of cold water. They dashed towards a nearby parking lot, the sound of sirens echoing in the distance. Lena's hand was still clasped in his, a lifeline amidst the chaos.

"Where should we go?" she gasped, glancing back nervously.

"Follow me," Sam urged, scanning the area. He spotted a line of motorcycles parked nearby. "I'll take one of those!"

He led her to the closest motorcycle, his heart pounding with the urgency of the moment. He quickly checked the ignition and was relieved to find it unlocked. He swung a leg over the seat and gestured for Lena to join him.

"Hold on tight!" he instructed, and she climbed on behind him, wrapping her arms around his waist.

As he revved the engine, the sound echoed into the night. With one last glance back at the chaos behind them, Sam sped out of the parking lot, the wind whipping against their faces as they raced down the darkened streets.

The adrenaline coursed through him, but beneath it lay a fierce protectiveness for Lena. He could feel her warmth pressed against his back, and the thrill of their escape mingled with the tension in the air.

A New Bond

They weaved through the streets, the city lights blurring into streaks of color. Sam navigated the winding roads, determined to find a place where they could regroup and catch their breath. As they rode, he could feel Lena's grip tightening around him, her body pressed against his—a connection forged in the heat of adrenaline and fear.

Eventually, they pulled over at a secluded beach, the waves crashing softly against the shore. Sam killed the engine, and they both dismounted, breathless and shaken.

Chapter 3: The Inciting Incident of Lena Disappearing

The cool breeze off the ocean felt refreshing against Sam's flushed skin as he and Lena stepped away from the motorcycle. The chaotic night was still fresh in their minds, and as they took a moment to collect themselves, the sound of crashing waves mingled with the distant echoes of sirens fading into the night.

"What just happened?" Lena breathed, her eyes wide with shock. "Was that really a shooting? I can't believe we just escaped that."

"I know," Sam replied, rubbing the back of his neck, still trying to process the whirlwind of events. "But we're safe now. That's what matters." He turned to her, wanting to comfort her, but her expression shifted from shock to something more complicated.

Lena took a deep breath, her eyes glistening under the moonlight. "I need to check on my friends," she said, her voice trembling. "They were still inside when we left. What if something happened to them?"

"Lena, it's not safe to go back right now," Sam urged, his protective instincts kicking in. "Let's get somewhere secure, and we can figure this out."

She shook her head, her determination evident. "I can't just leave them. I need to know they're okay."

Sam understood her urgency but couldn't shake the fear that lingered in the pit of his stomach. "Okay, let's find a phone. We can try to reach them."

A Disturbing Call

With that goal in mind, they walked along the beach toward a nearby lifeguard station, hoping to find a phone or a way to contact someone. The moon illuminated the path ahead, casting an ethereal glow on the sand, but the beauty of the night felt overshadowed by the tension in the air.

As they approached the lifeguard station, Lena pulled out her phone. "I'll try to call them," she said, her fingers trembling as she navigated through her contacts. Sam could see the worry etched on her face, and it twisted something deep inside him.

"Do you have their numbers?" he asked gently, wanting to help.

"I thought I did, but I can't remember everyone's names," she replied, frustration creeping into her voice. "I was just so excited to be there, and now..." Her voice trailed off, and Sam felt a pang of empathy for her distress.

He watched as she dialed a number and waited, her gaze fixed on the horizon. The waves crashed rhythmically, creating an unsettling soundtrack to their anxiety. Finally, the line connected, and Lena's expression brightened for a moment.

"Come on, pick up," she whispered, her eyes pleading. But as the ringing continued without an answer, her hope began to falter.

"Lena, it might be better to wait until things settle down," Sam suggested, placing a hand on her shoulder in an attempt to offer comfort. "Let's find a place to hide until we know it's safe."

Suddenly, her phone buzzed in her hand. She glanced at the screen, and her face turned pale. "It's a message from one of my friends!" Her voice was filled with urgency.

"What does it say?" Sam leaned closer, heart racing.

Lena read the message aloud, her voice shaking. "Lena, we're trapped! There's someone inside the venue, and they're looking for you. Get out of there now!"

The words hit Sam like a punch to the gut. "What do you mean, looking for you?" he asked, fear creeping into his voice.

"I don't know! I have to go back. I can't leave my friends!" She started to turn, but Sam grabbed her arm.

"No! You can't go back there! It's too dangerous!" he insisted, his grip firm but gentle. "We have to think this through."

Lena's eyes flashed with desperation. "But if they're in danger, I can't just stand here!"

The Dilemma

As the tension between them built, Sam felt the weight of the decision pressing heavily on his shoulders. He knew he had to keep her safe, but he could also see how deeply her loyalty to her friends ran.

"Lena," he said slowly, trying to keep his voice calm, "we need to think strategically. If someone's actively looking for you, going back might put you in even greater danger. We can alert the police or find another way to help them."

She hesitated, her mind racing. "What if they get hurt because I didn't go back? What if..." Her voice broke off, and Sam could see the internal battle she was facing.

"Then let's go to a police station, somewhere they can help," he suggested. "You can report what's happening, and they can send someone in. You don't have to do this alone."

Lena's shoulders slumped, her resolve faltering. "Okay," she said finally, her voice barely above a whisper. "Let's find help."

Relieved, Sam guided her back to the motorcycle, his protective instincts kicking in again. They mounted the bike, and he fired up the engine, revving it in anticipation. As they sped off, the cold air whipped around them, and Sam felt the adrenaline pulsing through his veins. He focused on the road ahead, his thoughts racing as he planned their next steps.

A Tense Ride

The ride to the nearest police station felt like an eternity, the quiet of the night only amplifying the tension between them. Sam glanced back at Lena, who sat behind him, her grip tight around his waist, her face a mask of worry. He could feel her heart racing against his back, and it echoed his own unease.

"Just hang on," he shouted over the roar of the motorcycle. "We're almost there."

As they approached the station, Sam felt a mix of relief and dread. They would be safe, but the reality of the situation weighed heavily on them both. He parked the motorcycle and they rushed inside, the fluorescent lights illuminating their anxious faces.

A police officer at the front desk looked up as they entered, concern washing over his features. "What can I do for you?" he asked, noticing the urgency in their demeanor.

"There's been a shooting at the gala," Sam said, breathless. "My friend's inside, and someone's looking for her. We need help!"

The officer nodded, taking immediate action. "Get me the details," he said, reaching for a notepad. "What's your name?"

"I'm Dr. Sam Cross, and this is Lena Hart. We were at the gala, and—"

"Lena Hart?" the officer interrupted, looking up sharply. "We've received reports about a woman by that name being targeted. We need you to stay calm and give us as much information as possible."

Sam exchanged a worried glance with Lena, who appeared pale but resolute. "I can tell you everything I know," she said, her voice steady despite the fear in her eyes. "We need to act quickly."

A Shocking Revelation

As they provided the officer with details about the gala and Lena's friends, Sam felt a knot tighten in his stomach. He watched Lena's expression shift from fear to determination as she recounted the events leading up to their escape.

Just as they finished, another officer burst into the room, his face grim. "We have a situation. A report just came in about a woman matching Lena's description. She's been taken from the venue."

"What?" Sam exclaimed, disbelief washing over him. "No, that can't be true!"

Lena gasped, her hands shaking as she pressed her palms against the desk. "What do you mean, taken? Who would do that?"

"We don't know yet," the officer replied, his tone serious. "But we have units responding to the scene. We need to keep you safe. You're a potential target."

Lena's eyes widened, panic seeping in. "I can't believe this is happening. I need to help my friends!"

"We'll do everything we can," the officer assured her. "But right now, we need to focus on getting you secured."

Sam's heart raced as he processed the implications of what was happening. They were running out of time, and Lena was in the crosshairs of a dangerous game. "What can we do?" he asked, his voice steady, determined to help Lena find a way through this nightmare.

The Escape Plan

The officers quickly devised a plan. They would escort Lena to a safe house while simultaneously trying to locate her friends inside the venue. Sam insisted on accompanying Lena, wanting to protect her at all costs.

As they prepared to leave, Lena turned to him, her eyes filled with gratitude and fear. "Thank you for being here, Sam. I don't know what I would do without you."

"Let's just focus on getting through this," he replied, his mind racing with strategies to keep them both safe.

They left the police station under the cover of darkness, police vehicles surrounding them as they made their way to a secure location. Sam's thoughts raced. He was determined to uncover the truth behind the chaos of the night and protect Lena from the unseen threats lurking in the shadows.

As they arrived at the safe house, a sense of urgency washed over him. He knew this was only the beginning of a tangled web of danger and deceit, and he would do everything in his power to help Lena navigate it.

Shadows of the Past

Once inside the safe house, Sam took a moment to assess their surroundings. It was a modest home, with bare walls and minimal furnishings, but it was fortified with security measures that made it feel safer than the chaos outside.

Lena paced the small living room, her anxious energy palpable. "I can't believe this is happening."

Chapter 4: Investigation

The safe house felt suffocating as Sam paced the modest living room, his mind racing. The walls, though adorned with simple art, felt like they were closing in, mirroring the tension that had built up inside him since that fateful night at the gala. He glanced at Lena, who sat on the worn sofa, her fingers anxiously tracing the outline of her phone. The gravity of the situation weighed heavily on them both.

"Do you have any idea who might be behind this?" Sam finally asked, breaking the silence that hung in the air like a heavy fog.

Lena shook her head, her brow furrowed in concentration. "I don't know. I've been trying to think of anyone who would want to hurt me, but nothing makes sense. The gala was supposed to be a celebration, not a nightmare."

Sam leaned against the wall, crossing his arms. "We need to dig deeper. There must be someone in your life—an ex, a competitor, anyone who might have a motive." He forced himself to remain calm, focusing on the task at hand despite the swirling emotions inside him.

"I've had my fair share of conflict in the tech world," Lena admitted, her voice trembling slightly. "But I've always kept my head down. I thought that if I worked hard, I could rise above the drama."

"That might have made you a target," Sam replied gently. "And the fact that someone was looking for you at the gala suggests they know you well enough to want to find you."

Lena sighed, her shoulders slumping. "I didn't think I had any enemies. I mean, everyone in Silicon Valley seems to play the game, but I've tried to keep things professional. This is all so unreal."

Sam pushed himself off the wall, determination igniting in his chest. "Then we'll figure it out together. I can help you with the psychological aspects, and I'll look into the situation from a more investigative angle. Let's find out who might want to hurt you."

Diving into the Investigation

With a plan taking shape, Sam grabbed his laptop from his bag, setting it up on the small dining table in the corner of the room. The glow of the screen illuminated the darkness as he began to type furiously, pulling up everything he could find about Lena and the gala. He needed a clear picture of the events leading up to the incident, as well as any potential threats lurking in Lena's professional sphere.

"Start from the beginning," he said, turning back to Lena. "Can you tell me everything that happened before the gala?"

She took a deep breath, collecting her thoughts. "I had a few meetings leading up to the event, networking with potential investors for my app. There was a lot of buzz around it, but not everyone was pleased with my approach. Some people in the industry can be... ruthless."

"Anyone stand out to you?" Sam asked, jotting down notes as she spoke.

"Actually, yes," Lena replied, her brow furrowing as she recalled the events. "There was a competitor, Mark Lawson, who's been trying to launch a similar product. He's been vocal about his disdain for me in the past. I didn't think much of it until now, but I suppose it's possible he could have something to gain from my disappearance."

"Let's dig into Mark's background," Sam suggested, his fingers flying over the keyboard as he pulled up information on the man. "If he's involved, we'll find evidence of it."

Unraveling Connections

As the minutes turned into hours, they worked side by side, sharing insights and uncovering details that might lead to the truth. Sam discovered that Mark Lawson was a well-known figure in the tech world, with a string of failed ventures and a history of aggressive tactics. He had a reputation for not playing by the rules, which only heightened Sam's concern.

"Lena, do you have any recent communications with him?" Sam asked, glancing up from his screen.

Lena hesitated, her eyes clouding with worry. "I... I received a few emails from him, but they were mostly business-related. Nothing too alarming. Let me check."

She rifled through her phone and pulled up a message thread, her fingers flying over the screen. "Here it is," she said, her voice dropping. "He reached out a week ago asking to meet up to discuss our projects. I declined, saying I was busy. I thought it was just another attempt to undermine me."

"That could be significant," Sam mused, his brow furrowing as he read through the messages. "Did you notice any tone in his messages that felt threatening?"

Lena considered it for a moment. "Not really. But I could tell he was frustrated. I mean, who wouldn't be? I've been stealing the spotlight lately."

"Let's look into his associates too," Sam suggested, feeling the puzzle pieces start to come together. "Anyone who might be connected to him could give us a clearer picture."

Lena nodded, her expression shifting from worry to focus. "I know a few people he collaborates with. We could check their social media profiles and see if they've been posting anything unusual."

Social Media Sleuthing

As they delved into the digital realm of social media, Lena's previous apprehension morphed into determination. The two worked seamlessly, each clicking through profiles, hunting for clues that could lead them to answers. The hours passed quickly, with each discovery igniting their hope of unraveling the mystery.

"Look at this," Lena said suddenly, pointing at the screen. "Mark just posted a picture from the gala. He's posing with some high-profile investors. It seems a little... too staged, don't you think?"

Sam leaned closer, squinting at the screen. "Yeah, it does. Like he's trying to position himself as a player in the game. This might not mean much, but let's see who else was tagged in this post."

They began to explore the profiles of the other attendees, hoping to find something that would connect the dots. As they scrolled through photos and comments, Lena's expression darkened. "There's someone else here I didn't expect to see," she said, her voice trembling slightly.

"Who?" Sam asked, his pulse quickening.

"It's Rachel Morgan," Lena replied, her eyes narrowing. "She's an investor I thought I could trust. We've had some late-night meetings about my app, but recently, she seemed... distant. I thought it was just her busy schedule, but now I'm not so sure."

"Let's look into her background," Sam said, feeling a surge of urgency. "She might have more connections to Mark than you realize."

As they explored Rachel's social media, they uncovered a trail of interactions with Mark that painted a picture of a potential partnership. Sam's gut twisted at the thought. "If they're working together, they could both have a motive to harm you."

Lena nodded, the fear returning to her features. "This is getting more complicated. I thought I was just dealing with one person, but now it feels like I'm at the center of something much bigger."

The Underlying Threat

The more they uncovered, the more Sam felt the weight of the situation pressing down on them. He wanted to protect Lena, but he also needed to confront the truth about the potential dangers she faced.

"I think we need to talk to Rachel," he said finally. "If she's involved, we need to find out where her loyalties lie."

Lena's eyes widened. "You want me to confront her? After everything that's happened?"

"We'll approach it carefully," Sam assured her. "But we can't ignore the possibility that she might be involved. We need to know where she stands before we proceed."

Lena took a deep breath, her anxiety evident. "Okay. But how do we do this without raising suspicion? I don't want to tip her off if she's connected to Mark."

"I'll help you formulate a plan," Sam replied, his mind already racing with ideas. "We can set up a casual meeting, act like everything is normal, and then see if she slips up."

As they discussed their strategy, Sam couldn't shake the feeling that time was running out. With each passing hour, the threat loomed larger, and the need to protect Lena intensified. They needed answers, and they needed them fast.

A Calculated Risk

After some brainstorming, they agreed to arrange a meeting with Rachel under the guise of discussing investment opportunities for Lena's app. "This way, we can keep things light," Sam suggested. "If she senses any tension, she might become defensive, and we need her to feel comfortable."

Lena nodded, but uncertainty flickered in her eyes. "What if she doesn't respond well? What if she sees through our ruse?"

"Then we'll adapt," Sam replied, his determination unwavering. "We'll be on guard and ready for anything. Just remember to trust your instincts."

They formulated a message to Rachel, inviting her for coffee at a nearby café known for its discretion. "I'll send this now," Lena said, her fingers trembling slightly as she hit send. "Now we wait."

The anticipation hung in the air, and Sam could feel the tension coursing between them. He wanted to reassure her, to tell her that everything would be okay, but the reality of the situation weighed heavily on his heart. He couldn't shake the feeling that they were venturing deeper into a labyrinth of danger.

A Day of Reckoning

The following day dawned with an unsettling stillness. Sam and Lena had agreed to meet Rachel at 10 a.m. The café buzzed with the sound of espresso machines and muffled conversations, a stark contrast to the turmoil churning inside them.

Chapter 5: Flashbacks

The sun streamed through the window of the safe house, casting soft patterns of light across the small living room where Sam and Lena sat in tense silence. Lena stared out at the ocean, her thoughts a storm of anxiety and anticipation as they awaited Rachel's response. But as the waves crashed against the shore, a different kind of wave surged through her—a tide of memories that threatened to pull her under.

In that moment, Lena's mind drifted back to a summer long ago, a time when the world felt brighter, yet shadows lingered just beneath the surface.

A Childhood Moment

Lena was ten years old, playing in her backyard under the warm sun of a suburban afternoon. The air was thick with the scent of freshly cut grass and blooming flowers. She laughed with her friends as they chased each other around the swing set, the joy of childhood wrapping around her like a warm blanket.

"Catch me if you can!" she shouted, sprinting toward the tall oak tree that stood sentinel at the edge of the yard. Her heart raced, the thrill of the chase fueling her energy.

But the laughter faded as a figure stepped into her line of sight—a man standing just beyond the fence, watching her with an unsettling intensity. His eyes were cold, his expression unreadable. Lena skidded to a halt, the smile fading from her face as an instinctual fear gripped her.

"Who are you?" she called out, her voice trembling slightly.

The man didn't respond. He simply stood there, a dark silhouette against the vibrant backdrop of her childhood, and as she took a step back, the laughter of her friends faded away, replaced by an eerie silence.

"Lena! Come back!" Her friend Sarah's voice pierced through the tension, breaking her trance. But Lena was already retreating, her instincts screaming at her to run.

Confronting Fears

Lena's breath quickened as the memory faded, the laughter replaced by the haunting chill of that moment. She had always thought of herself as brave, but even now, that fear lingered in her bones.

"Lena?" Sam's voice cut through her thoughts, pulling her back to the present. "Are you okay?"

She blinked, the reality of their situation crashing back in. "Yeah, I'm fine," she lied, forcing a smile. "Just... lost in thought."

"Do you want to talk about it?" he asked gently, concern etched across his features.

She shook her head, unwilling to dive into the depths of her memories. "It's nothing I can't handle. I'm just... anxious about meeting Rachel."

But the truth was, anxiety wasn't just about the meeting; it was about everything—the gala, the shooting, and the memories that haunted her.

Family Torn Apart

As she fought to keep her thoughts at bay, another memory surfaced, unbidden and unwelcome.

Lena was fifteen, sitting at the kitchen table with her parents. The atmosphere was thick with tension, her father's face flushed with anger. "You can't keep doing this, Lena!" he shouted, his voice booming against the walls. "You need to focus on your studies, not on these ridiculous friends of yours!"

Her mother sat quietly, eyes downcast, as Lena felt the familiar tightening in her chest. She wanted to scream, to argue back, but all that came out was a shaky breath.

"I'm trying to make friends, Dad! I just want to fit in!" she replied, her voice cracking under the weight of her emotions.

"You need to prioritize what's important. This isn't a game!" he barked, slamming his fist on the table, causing the plates to rattle.

At that moment, the door swung open, and her older brother, Matt, rushed in, breathless. "What's going on?"

"Nothing that concerns you!" their father shot back, his voice laced with disdain.

But it did concern Matt. "It's always something with you, Dad!" he retorted. "Can't you see you're pushing her away?"

The argument spiraled out of control, voices raised and words thrown like daggers. Lena felt the weight of her father's anger, the suffocating pressure that made it hard to breathe. In that moment, she realized that her family, once her safe haven, was crumbling before her eyes.

The Weight of the Past

Lena shook her head, trying to dispel the images of her past. The memories of that summer and the fights with her father had shaped her in ways she was only beginning to understand. They had instilled in her a fear of confrontation, a desire to please those around her at the cost of her own happiness.

"Lena, are you sure you're okay?" Sam's voice broke through her thoughts again, more insistent this time.

"I'm fine," she repeated, but the tremor in her voice betrayed her. She knew she needed to confront these feelings, but doing so felt like standing on the edge of a precipice, staring into an abyss.

"I just..." she began, her voice faltering. "I just don't want to go back to that place where everything feels out of control."

Sam nodded, his expression softening. "I get it. But you're not alone this time. You have me."

His words offered a small comfort, but the shadows of her past clung to her like a second skin. She had spent so long trying to bury those memories, but now they felt like chains, binding her to a reality she couldn't escape.

The Defining Moment

The memories surged again, this time pulling her into the darkest recesses of her past.

It was her senior year of high school, and the anxiety had reached a breaking point. She had worked tirelessly to maintain her grades, to please her parents, but the pressure felt like a vice around her chest. It all came to a head one afternoon in the school hallway.

"Lena, are you okay?" Sarah asked, concern etched on her face.

"Yeah, I'm fine," Lena replied, forcing a smile that felt like a mask.

But Sarah wasn't convinced. "You don't look fine. You look exhausted. You can't keep pushing yourself like this."

"I have to! My dad expects me to be perfect!" Lena snapped, the frustration spilling over.

Sarah's eyes widened. "Lena, you need to take a break. You can't keep doing this to yourself."

But Lena didn't want to hear it. "I can't afford to take a break! I have to get into a good college!"

That night, the weight of her emotions finally caught up with her. Alone in her room, the tears flowed freely as she struggled to reconcile the expectations of her family with her own desires. It felt like she was drowning, caught in a whirlpool of anxiety and despair.

That was the night she made a decision. She wouldn't let anyone dictate her life anymore. She wouldn't be the perfect daughter or the perfect student; she would find a way to carve out her own path, even if it meant confronting her deepest fears.

Facing the Truth

As the flashback faded, Lena felt a surge of determination. She had come too far to let the ghosts of her past dictate her future. She would face Rachel, not as the scared girl she once was, but as a woman who had fought to reclaim her life.

"I'm ready," she said softly, meeting Sam's gaze. "I need to do this. I can't let fear control me any longer."

Sam smiled, pride shining in his eyes. "That's the spirit. Just remember, you're not alone in this. We'll get through it together."

But as Lena took a deep breath, she couldn't shake the lingering fear that the past would rear its ugly head again. She had fought hard to escape the grip of her childhood traumas, but now, with danger lurking just beyond the horizon, she felt those shadows creeping closer once more.

A Glimpse of Darkness

The night of her high school graduation, Lena felt like she was finally free. The ceremony had been a blur of smiles and laughter, and as she celebrated with friends, she couldn't shake the feeling of impending doom that gnawed at her.

Later that evening, as the parties kicked off, Lena found herself alone in the backyard, staring at the stars. That's when she heard the voices—the hushed tones of her parents arguing, the sharpness of her father's words cutting through the air.

"Why can't you see what she's doing to herself?" her mother cried, desperation lacing her voice. "She's trying so hard, and you keep pushing her!"

"She needs to toughen up," her father snapped. "Life isn't a game, and she needs to learn that!"

The exchange shattered her heart. All she had ever wanted was to make them proud, but the constant pressure had turned her family into a battleground. It felt like a knife twisting in her gut, the realization that love had become conditional.

Embracing Strength

Lena turned away from the memory, her chest tight with the familiar ache of her past. But in that moment, something shifted within her. She had survived the storm, and she had emerged stronger, more resilient. She would not let Rachel—or anyone—intimidate her again.

"I won't back down," she whispered, more to herself than to Sam. "I will face Rachel, and I will demand the truth."

Sam nodded, his expression unwavering. "That's the spirit. Let's prepare ourselves. I'll be right by your side."

Together, they gathered their things, Lena's heart racing.

Chapter 6: Reconnect

The café was alive with chatter and the rich aroma of coffee as Sam and Lena settled into a secluded corner booth. The atmosphere felt both inviting and oppressive, a stark contrast to the storm brewing inside Lena's heart. She glanced at the clock, her anxiety rising as they awaited Rachel's arrival. The world felt heavy with unspoken words, and every tick of the clock echoed her fears.

"I wish she'd hurry up," Lena muttered, fidgeting with the hem of her sweater.

"She'll be here," Sam reassured her, his eyes scanning the bustling café for any sign of Rachel. "Just focus on the plan. Remember, we're just here to gather information."

Lena nodded, but the unease clawed at her insides. Her heart raced at the thought of facing Rachel, the woman she once viewed as a mentor, now potentially entangled in a web of deceit. Would she be able to confront her and find the truth they so desperately needed?

Before she could spiral further into her thoughts, Sam leaned in closer. "Hey, why don't we go over what we know about Rachel again? It might help to solidify our approach."

Lena took a deep breath, her thoughts racing. "Okay. She's been an investor in the tech scene for years, and she was really supportive when I first started. But lately, she's seemed distant, almost dismissive. I've sensed a shift in her attitude."

Sam nodded, his expression serious. "And we suspect she has ties to Mark Lawson. That's crucial. If she's involved in any way, we need to handle this delicately."

"Right," Lena said, recalling the countless late-night meetings they'd had over the past year, when Rachel had seemed genuinely interested in her app. "She was always enthusiastic about my ideas, but it felt different lately. Like she was more focused on her own interests than mine."

"Let's use that," Sam suggested. "When she arrives, we can start by discussing your project. See if she brings up Mark, or if she shows any signs of discomfort."

As they reviewed their plan, Lena felt a flicker of hope. Maybe they could unravel the truth together, piece by piece, like a puzzle slowly revealing its image.

Rachel Arrives

Just then, the door swung open, and Rachel walked in, her presence commanding and polished as ever. She wore a fitted blazer that accentuated her silhouette, her dark hair slicked back into a neat bun. Lena felt a chill run down her spine as their eyes met. This was the woman who had once inspired her, now a potential threat lurking in the shadows.

"Lena! Sam!" Rachel called, her voice smooth and warm as she approached their table. "So good to see you both!"

"Thanks for meeting us, Rachel," Lena said, forcing a smile as she motioned for her to join them.

"Of course! I've been meaning to catch up," Rachel replied, sliding into the booth with a practiced ease. "I've heard amazing things about your app, Lena. The tech world is buzzing!"

"Really?" Lena replied, masking her skepticism. "I'm glad to hear that. I've been working hard on it."

Rachel's gaze flickered to Sam, and for a brief moment, Lena thought she detected a hint of tension in her expression. "And what about you, Sam? Still diving into the world of psychology?"

"Yes, I am," he replied, his tone friendly yet measured. "I'm actually here to support Lena during this project. It's an exciting time for her."

"Support is important," Rachel said, nodding thoughtfully. "Especially in such a competitive field. It's good to see you two collaborating."

A Subtle Dance of Words

As they settled into small talk, Lena's pulse quickened. She had to navigate this conversation carefully, all while watching for any signs that Rachel was hiding something.

"So, Lena, tell me about the latest developments with your app," Rachel prompted, leaning forward, her interest seemingly genuine.

Lena took a breath, launching into her pitch. "Well, I've incorporated some new features that I think will really set it apart from the competition. It's designed to create a personalized experience for users, helping them engage with technology in a more intuitive way."

"That sounds fantastic," Rachel replied, her eyes sparkling with interest. "You've really thought this through. How do you plan to market it?"

"Honestly, I'm still figuring that part out," Lena admitted, glancing at Sam for support. "That's why I wanted to get your perspective. I know you have a lot of experience in the industry."

Rachel smiled, but there was a tightness in her expression. "I'd be happy to offer my thoughts. Marketing can be tricky, especially when there are so many players in the game."

Lena seized the moment. "Speaking of competition, what do you think about Mark Lawson's recent push into the market? His app is getting a lot of attention."

Rachel's demeanor shifted ever so slightly, and Lena noted the tightening of her jaw. "Mark is ambitious, that's for sure. But ambition can lead to mistakes. I've seen it happen before."

"Do you think he poses a threat?" Sam asked, his tone casual but probing.

Rachel's eyes flickered, a brief flash of irritation crossing her face before she regained her composure. "In business, there's always a threat. But I believe in the strength of my investments."

Lena felt the tension rise as she pushed forward. "I've heard rumors that Mark has been trying to undermine competitors. It seems like the industry is becoming increasingly cutthroat."

Rachel leaned back in her seat, her expression carefully neutral. "Well, that's the nature of the beast. People will do what they need to succeed." Her eyes met Lena's, and in that moment, Lena felt a chill. It was a veiled warning, a reminder of the harsh realities they were navigating.

Piecing Together Clues

Sam exchanged a glance with Lena, sensing the shift in the conversation. "Lena and I have been exploring different avenues to improve the app's launch strategy," he said, trying to steer the discussion back to safer ground. "What do you think about leveraging social media influencers?"

Rachel perked up slightly, her interest rekindled. "That could work, especially if you can find the right fit for your brand. But you need to be cautious; influencers can be a double-edged sword."

"Exactly," Lena said, grateful for the momentary distraction. "I want to ensure that any partnerships align with my vision and values."

Rachel nodded, a hint of approval creeping into her expression. "That's a wise approach. You don't want to compromise your integrity just for the sake of exposure."

Navigating the Conversation

As the conversation flowed, Lena felt the unease beneath the surface. Rachel was skilled at redirecting, keeping the conversation focused on business while avoiding the more personal aspects. It felt like a dance—one wrong step, and the entire façade could come crashing down.

"Have you had a chance to catch up with Mark recently?" Lena asked, testing the waters. "I heard he was trying to recruit talent from various startups."

Rachel's smile faltered for just a moment. "I haven't spoken to him in a while. I prefer to keep my distance from anyone who plays those kinds of games." Her tone was sharp, the underlying hostility unmistakable.

Lena's heart raced as she pushed further. "What do you mean by 'games'?"

Rachel's gaze turned icy. "You know how it is in this industry. Some people thrive on manipulation. I choose to focus on building genuine connections."

"Genuine connections," Lena echoed, feeling the weight of those words. "Is that why you've distanced yourself from me lately? I thought we had a strong connection."

Rachel's expression shifted, and for a brief moment, Lena saw a flicker of vulnerability. "It's complicated, Lena. The industry isn't as simple as it seems."

The Moment of Truth

As the conversation reached a boiling point, Lena felt a surge of determination. "Rachel, I need to know if you're truly on my side. There's been too much at stake for me to ignore the possibility that something darker is happening here."

Rachel's eyes narrowed, the mask slipping. "What are you insinuating?"

"I'm not insinuating anything," Lena replied, her voice steady. "I'm asking for clarity. If there's any chance you're aligned with Mark, I need to know. My life may depend on it."

The tension in the air thickened, and for a moment, it felt like the world around them had disappeared. Rachel's composure wavered, and Lena could see the internal struggle playing out in her eyes.

"I would never align myself with someone like Mark," Rachel said finally, her voice low but fierce. "But I won't deny that the industry is fraught with danger. If you're in the crosshairs, you need to be vigilant."

"Then help me," Lena pleaded, her heart pounding. "Help me understand what's really going on."

A Fragile Alliance

Rachel took a deep breath, visibly weighing her options. "I can't promise you anything. But I'll keep an ear to the ground. There are whispers in the industry, and I'll see what I can find out."

"Thank you," Lena said, relief washing over her. "That's all I ask."

As they wrapped up their meeting, Lena felt a sense of cautious optimism. She and Sam had navigated a precarious conversation, uncovering pieces of a puzzle that still felt incomplete. But with Rachel potentially on their side—if only for her own interests—they had a new lead.

Chapter 7: Tension Builds

The air in the café had shifted, the once vibrant atmosphere now overshadowed by an uneasy tension. Sam felt it the moment Rachel stood to leave, the subtle change in her demeanor a silent alarm. As she exchanged polite farewells with Lena, he couldn't shake the feeling that their conversation had crossed an unseen line.

"Let's keep in touch," Rachel said, a tight smile playing on her lips. "And remember, Lena, this industry can be as ruthless as it is rewarding."

Lena nodded, her gaze lingering on Rachel as she slipped out of the café. Sam could sense the worry in her expression, the unease that had settled deep within her. He reached across the table, placing his hand over hers.

"We'll figure this out," he assured her. "Together."

Lena offered a faint smile, but Sam could see the shadows lurking in her eyes. They gathered their things, the weight of their conversation pressing heavily on their shoulders as they stepped outside.

The sun hung low in the sky, casting long shadows across the sidewalk. As they walked back to Sam's car, he couldn't shake the feeling that they were being watched.

The Drive Home

Once inside the car, Sam turned the key in the ignition, and the engine roared to life. "Where to?" he asked, glancing at Lena, who was staring out the window, lost in thought.

"Home, I guess," she replied, her voice distant.

"Okay. We'll review everything we learned later," he said, trying to inject some normalcy into the atmosphere. "I think we've made significant progress."

Lena nodded absently, and as they drove through the bustling streets, Sam couldn't help but feel a growing sense of urgency. The revelations they had gleaned from Rachel were critical, but it was clear there was more at play.

As they turned onto a quieter street, a glimmer of movement caught Sam's eye. He glanced in the rearview mirror, his heart dropping as he noticed a dark SUV trailing closely behind them.

"Lena," he said, his voice tense. "I think we're being followed."

She turned sharply, her expression shifting from contemplative to alarmed. "What? Are you sure?"

"Yeah," he confirmed, trying to remain calm. "Just stay quiet."

Sam tightened his grip on the steering wheel, his instincts kicking into overdrive. He merged into a side street, hoping to lose the vehicle behind them. The SUV mirrored his movements, its headlights cutting through the fading light like a predator stalking its prey.

The Chase Begins

Panic surged through Sam as he pressed the accelerator, urging his car to speed up. "I need you to stay calm," he said, glancing at Lena, who was gripping the edge of her seat. "If it comes to it, I'll find a way to get us out of this."

Lena nodded, but the fear in her eyes was unmistakable. "What do you think they want?"

"Maybe they're connected to Rachel," Sam speculated, weaving through traffic. "Or perhaps they're after you because of Mark Lawson."

"Whoever they are, we need to lose them," Lena urged, her voice steadier now.

Sam turned onto a narrow alleyway, praying it would lead them to safety. The SUV pursued them relentlessly, its engine roaring as it closed the gap. "Hold on!" Sam shouted, making a sharp turn onto a busier street, hoping the sudden change would give them a chance to break free.

The sound of honking horns and screeching tires filled the air as they re-entered the main road. Sam glanced in the rearview mirror again, his heart sinking as the SUV swerved to follow, its driver clearly skilled at the chase.

"Take the next left!" Lena shouted, pointing to an intersection ahead.

Sam didn't hesitate, turning sharply once more, his instincts guiding him. He could feel the adrenaline coursing through his veins, sharpening his senses as he navigated the chaotic streets.

A Desperate Escape

The SUV stayed on their tail, relentless and aggressive. Sam took another turn, the tires squealing in protest as he pushed the car to its limits. "We need a plan," he said, his mind racing.

"Where are we headed?" Lena asked, her voice filled with urgency.

"Somewhere busy," Sam replied, searching for a way to blend into the crowd. "We need to lose them in a place where they can't just follow us."

As they approached a bustling downtown area, the streets filled with pedestrians and evening shoppers, Sam felt a flicker of hope. "There!" he pointed to a parking garage up ahead. "We can lose them in there."

"Do it!" Lena urged.

Sam slammed on the brakes, turning sharply into the parking garage entrance. The SUV followed, its headlights flashing as they entered the dimly lit structure. Sam scanned for an open spot, his heart racing as he navigated the maze of concrete pillars and parked cars.

"Keep an eye out for them," he said, glancing at Lena. "We need to find a place to hide."

As he pulled into a secluded corner, he shut off the engine and turned off the headlights, plunging them into darkness. They both held their breath, listening intently as the sound of the SUV's engine echoed through the garage.

"What if they find us?" Lena whispered, her voice trembling.

"They won't," Sam said, trying to instill confidence in her. "We just have to stay quiet and wait."

The Tension Rises

As they sat in silence, the atmosphere thick with anxiety, Sam's mind raced with possibilities. Who were these people? What did they want? He glanced at Lena, her face pale, eyes wide with fear.

"Hey," he said softly, reaching for her hand. "We'll get through this. Just stay with me."

Lena squeezed his hand, her expression one of determination. "I trust you, Sam."

The tension in the air seemed to vibrate with unspoken fears. Minutes passed like hours, the only sound their quiet breathing and the distant hum of the city outside.

Then, the engine of the SUV roared to life, and Sam felt his heart drop. They were still searching. He motioned for Lena to stay still as the sound of tires rolling over concrete grew louder. The SUV crept past their hiding spot, its headlights illuminating the rows of parked cars, casting eerie shadows on the walls.

"Stay low," Sam whispered, pulling Lena closer.

As the vehicle moved further away, Sam felt a mixture of relief and dread. They were still in danger, and he knew they couldn't stay here for long.

A New Plan

"I think we should make a break for it," Sam said quietly, glancing at Lena. "When they pass by again, we can slip out and head for the nearest exit."

Lena nodded, her expression serious. "But where do we go?"

"We need to find a public place—somewhere crowded. We can regroup and figure out our next steps," he suggested.

As they listened for the sound of the SUV retreating, Sam's mind raced. They needed to contact Rachel, but how could they do that safely? He pulled out his phone, checking for signal, but the reception was spotty in the garage.

Suddenly, the sound of the SUV echoed back into the garage, and Sam's heart raced. "They're coming back!" he hissed, pressing against the door, willing it to blend into the shadows.

"Just breathe," Lena urged, her voice barely above a whisper. "We'll find a way out."

As the SUV slowed to a halt, Sam's pulse quickened. He could see the dark shape through the windshield, the silhouette of a driver scanning the area, searching for them.

"We can't stay here," he said, gripping Lena's arm. "Now or never."

Making a Move

With a sudden burst of adrenaline, Sam opened the door slightly, peering out. The coast seemed clear for a moment, but the tension hung heavy in the air. He turned to Lena, his eyes fierce with determination. "On three."

Lena nodded, her breathing steadying. "One... two... three!"

They both slipped out of the car, crouching low and darting behind the nearest concrete pillar. Sam's heart raced as they crouched, listening for any sign that they had been spotted.

"Let's go!" he urged, motioning toward the exit. They moved quickly but cautiously, avoiding the open spaces where they could be easily seen.

As they approached the exit, Sam glanced back, hoping they wouldn't be followed. But just as they reached the door, the SUV roared to life again. The engine's growl echoed ominously in the garage, sending a fresh wave of panic through Sam.

"Run!" he shouted, and they sprinted toward the exit, adrenaline fueling their every step.

Into the Night

Bursting through the exit, they emerged into the night, the cool air hitting them like a wave of relief. Sam glanced around, spotting a group of people nearby. "We need to blend in," he said, pulling Lena toward the crowd.

They joined a throng of pedestrians walking down the street, the noise of laughter and chatter enveloping them. Sam's heart raced, but the presence of the crowd offered a semblance of safety.

"Do you see the SUV?" Lena asked, her eyes darting around.

"No," Sam replied, scanning the street for any sign of the pursuers. "Let's keep moving. We need to get to a safe place and figure out our next steps."

As they walked briskly, Sam felt a wave of relief wash over him.

Chapter 8: Romantic Getaway on a Yacht

The sun hung low on the horizon, casting a warm golden glow over the bay. Sam stood on the deck of the sleek yacht, the gentle sound of waves lapping against the hull creating a soothing melody. He took a deep breath, inhaling the salty air, feeling a sense of peace wash over him. This was the escape he and Lena desperately needed—a moment away from the chaos that had engulfed their lives.

"Isn't this incredible?" Lena called out, her voice filled with excitement as she stepped onto the deck, her hair blowing in the breeze. She wore a light sundress that danced around her knees, and the joy in her eyes made Sam's heart skip a beat.

"It really is," he replied, unable to keep the smile off his face as he took in the sight of her. The worry lines that had etched themselves on her face during their recent trials were fading, if only for a moment. "I can't believe we actually pulled this off."

"Thanks to Rachel," Lena said, her voice tinged with gratitude. "I still can't believe she offered us the yacht for the weekend. It was so generous of her."

Sam nodded, remembering the conversation that had led them here. After the harrowing chase through the parking garage, they had decided to reach out to Rachel, explaining their need for some time away to gather their thoughts. To their surprise, Rachel had agreed and offered them her luxurious yacht, docked just a short drive from the city.

"It was a good move to take her up on it," Sam said, his tone light. "We needed this break."

Lena smiled, and for a moment, they stood in comfortable silence, the sound of the water and the distant laughter of other boaters creating a serene backdrop. But as Sam glanced at the horizon, a tinge of unease flickered at the edges of his mind. They had only been free from their pursuers for a short while, and the shadows of their recent encounters still lingered.

"Are you okay?" Lena asked, her gaze searching his face.

"Yeah, just thinking," he said, forcing a smile. "It's beautiful here. I want to enjoy it while we can."

"Let's make the most of it," Lena said, her eyes sparkling with determination. "How about a swim? The water looks amazing."

A Splash of Fun

Sam chuckled, the idea bringing a welcome distraction. "Sure, but we should be cautious. We don't want to draw too much attention."

"Come on, Sam! A little fun won't hurt," Lena insisted, her enthusiasm infectious. "I'll race you to the water!"

Before he could protest, Lena dashed toward the edge of the boat, her laughter ringing out like music. Sam grinned, shaking his head as he followed her, the thrill of the moment washing over him. They stripped down to their swimsuits, the water's allure pulling them closer as they stood at the edge of the yacht.

"On your mark, get set, go!" Lena shouted, and they both dove into the crystalline water.

The cool embrace of the ocean was invigorating, washing away the stress of their recent troubles. They surfaced, spluttering and laughing, the sun glinting off the water around them.

"Not bad for a psychologist, huh?" Sam teased, swimming closer.

Lena smirked, playfully splashing him. "I'll have you know I was on the swim team in high school. I've got some serious skills."

"I'll believe it when I see it," he replied, grinning as he challenged her to another race.

As they swam, the competitive spirit ignited between them. They raced from one end of the boat to the other, the warm sun overhead and the refreshing water enveloping them in a sense of freedom.

An Intimate Moment

Eventually, they both climbed back onto the yacht, breathless and exhilarated. As they lounged on the deck, drying off in the sun, Sam felt a shift in the atmosphere. The weight of their recent struggles faded away, replaced by a burgeoning intimacy that felt electric.

"Can you believe we made it here?" Lena said, her eyes sparkling with excitement as she rested her head on her arms, looking at him.

"I know," Sam replied, feeling a warmth spread through him as he met her gaze. "It's like we're in a different world."

Lena smiled, her cheeks flushing slightly. "It's nice to escape, even if it's just for a little while."

"Definitely," Sam said, his heart racing as their eyes lingered on each other. "You deserve this. We both do."

As the sun dipped lower, painting the sky in shades of orange and pink, Lena propped herself up on her elbows. "What do you think is next for us?" she asked, her voice softer now.

"I don't know," Sam admitted, his heart pounding. "I guess we'll figure it out as we go."

"Do you think Rachel can help us with finding out what's really going on?" she asked, her brows knitting together in concern.

"I hope so," Sam said, trying to remain optimistic. "But for now, I just want to enjoy this moment with you."

Lena smiled, her eyes sparkling. "Me too."

As they basked in the fading sunlight, a sense of calm washed over them. They were far from the chaos of their lives, if only for a few precious hours.

An Unexpected Turn

As evening approached, Lena suggested they prepare dinner. The yacht's kitchen was small but well-equipped, and they had brought along a selection of ingredients. "Let's make it a proper evening," she said, her excitement infectious.

"Sounds like a plan," Sam agreed, his mind still buzzing with the day's events. They moved into the small kitchen, working together to chop vegetables and prepare a simple pasta dish. The warmth of the stove and the aroma of garlic filled the air, creating a cozy atmosphere.

"Do you think we'll be able to relax tonight?" Lena asked, glancing at Sam as they stirred the pot.

"I hope so," he replied, trying to shake off the lingering tension. "We deserve a break from everything."

As they chatted and laughed, the shadows of doubt began to lift, replaced by the intimacy of shared moments. Sam couldn't help but admire Lena's effortless grace, the way she moved about the small kitchen, her laughter infectious.

As they set the table on the deck, the sky transitioned from vibrant colors to deep indigos, the first stars beginning to twinkle overhead. They lit candles, the flickering flames casting a warm glow around them.

"Dinner is served," Lena announced playfully, placing the dishes on the table.

"Wow, it looks incredible," Sam said, genuinely impressed. "You've outdone yourself."

"Just wait until you taste it," she replied with a wink. They clinked their glasses together, the sound mingling with the gentle lapping of waves against the yacht.

The Calm Before the Storm

As they settled into their meal, Sam felt the tension of the past few days begin to melt away. They talked about everything and nothing, sharing stories and dreams, their laughter echoing in the quiet of the night.

"Do you remember that time we got stuck in the elevator during the conference?" Lena asked, her eyes bright with the memory. "I thought we'd never get out!"

"Of course," Sam laughed. "I still can't believe how panicked we both were. But I have to admit, it was a great bonding experience."

Lena leaned back in her chair, a thoughtful expression crossing her face. "I never would have imagined we'd end up here, on a yacht, after everything we've been through."

"Life is full of surprises," Sam said, his gaze steady on her. "And I'm glad I have you by my side through it all."

Lena's cheeks flushed slightly, and for a moment, the weight of the world seemed to vanish, leaving only the two of them under the starlit sky.

As they finished dinner, Sam felt a surge of affection for Lena. She had been through so much, yet she radiated strength and resilience. He reached across the table, taking her hand in his.

"Lena," he said softly, "I want you to know that I'm here for you. No matter what happens next, we'll face it together."

She squeezed his hand, her eyes shimmering with emotion. "Thank you, Sam. That means everything to me."

An Unexpected Visitor

Just as they finished cleaning up, the tranquility of their evening was abruptly shattered by the distant sound of an engine. Sam's heart sank as he glanced at the horizon, spotting the dark silhouette of a boat approaching.

"Do you see that?" he asked, his voice tense.

Lena turned, her expression shifting to concern. "What is that?"

"I don't know, but it looks like they're heading our way," Sam replied, a knot forming in his stomach.

As the boat drew closer, the engine's roar grew louder, and Sam felt the tension return. "We should stay alert," he said, scanning the approaching vessel for any signs of danger.

"What if it's just someone out for a late-night cruise?" Lena asked, trying to remain hopeful.

"Maybe," Sam said, but his instincts told him otherwise. There was something unsettling about the way the boat was cutting through the water, heading directly for them.

As the other boat neared, Sam could make out the figures on board. There were two men, their expressions masked by the shadows, and they seemed to be watching them closely.

"Lena, stay close," Sam instructed, his heart racing.

Chapter 9: A High-Stakes Car Chase

The tension on the yacht was palpable as the dark boat closed in on them. Sam's instincts kicked into overdrive; he could feel the threat radiating off the two men aboard the approaching vessel. The evening's tranquility shattered like glass, and he felt a protective instinct rise within him, urging him to shield Lena from whatever danger lay ahead.

"Sam, what do we do?" Lena whispered, her voice laced with fear.

"Stay calm," he said, his heart pounding. "We need to assess the situation first. Let's not panic."

As the other boat edged closer, Sam caught a glimpse of the men. Their expressions were grim, their eyes cold and calculating. He could see that one of them held something in his hand—an object that glinted ominously under the moonlight.

"I think they're armed," Sam muttered, his voice low.

Lena's eyes widened in horror. "What do we do?"

Sam glanced around the deck, searching for a plan. "We need to get off this yacht and to safety. If they're here for us, staying put is not an option."

Just then, the men on the approaching boat shouted something unintelligible, their voices muffled by the distance and the roar of their engine. But it was enough to send Sam's adrenaline spiking.

"Go!" he ordered, grabbing Lena's hand. "We need to move!"

A Leap into Action

With urgency in his stride, Sam led Lena down the steps into the cabin. They needed to find a way off the yacht, and quickly. He could hear the other boat's engine roaring as it closed the distance between them.

"Over here!" Lena exclaimed, pointing to a small inflatable dinghy tied to the side of the yacht.

"Good thinking!" Sam replied, dashing toward it. He quickly unfastened the ropes and began to inflate it with a small pump he noticed sitting nearby.

"Are you sure this is safe?" Lena asked, her eyes darting back to the approaching men.

"It's our best option right now," he said, glancing over his shoulder. The men were jumping off their boat and onto the yacht, their movements swift and determined.

"Let's go!" Sam shouted as the dinghy inflated enough for them to use.

They hopped in, and Sam grabbed the small oars, maneuvering the dinghy away from the yacht as fast as he could. The moonlight illuminated their escape, and for a fleeting moment, they felt the rush of hope.

Suddenly, he heard a loud splash behind them, and he turned just in time to see one of the men leap into the water, pursuing them. "They're coming!" he shouted.

"Row faster!" Lena urged, her voice filled with urgency.

Sam's muscles strained as he paddled harder, propelling the dinghy into the open water. But the man was a strong swimmer, gaining on them with every stroke. Just as panic began to creep in, Sam spotted the dark silhouette of their original boat still moored at the dock.

"If we can get to that boat, we'll have a chance!" Sam shouted, determination igniting within him.

A Desperate Escape

With renewed vigor, they raced towards the larger vessel. Sam's heart pounded as he pushed the dinghy forward, glancing back to see the man gaining on them. The distance between them was closing, and they needed to reach the boat before he caught up.

"Almost there!" Sam encouraged, pushing through the fatigue.

Just as they reached the larger boat, Sam quickly tied the dinghy off and helped Lena climb aboard. "Get inside!" he ordered, urgency lacing his tone.

Lena scrambled up the ladder, and Sam followed, his heart racing. They hurried inside the cabin, shutting the door behind them and locking it.

"Do you think he'll follow us?" Lena asked, her voice shaky.

"I hope not, but we can't wait around to find out," Sam replied, scanning the small cabin for anything they could use as a weapon. "Let's see what we've got here."

As he rummaged through drawers, he found a few life jackets and a flare gun. "This could be useful," he said, holding it up.

"Should we call for help?" Lena suggested, her eyes wide.

"There's no time for that," Sam said, his voice firm. "We need to get the boat started and get out of here."

Engine Trouble

Sam rushed to the control panel, quickly assessing the situation. "Come on, come on," he muttered, fumbling with the ignition switch. But nothing happened. Panic surged through him as he tried again, and again, but the engine remained silent.

"Sam!" Lena cried out, her voice edged with fear. "What's happening?"

"It's not starting," he admitted, desperation creeping into his voice. "We need to find another way."

Just then, a loud thud echoed from outside the cabin, and Sam's heart raced. The man had reached the yacht.

"Lena, hide!" he commanded, motioning for her to slip into a small storage compartment.

"No! I'm not leaving you!" she protested, her eyes filled with defiance.

"Please, for your safety," Sam insisted, his voice firm but pleading. "I need you to trust me."

With reluctance, Lena slipped into the compartment, and Sam closed the door just as the sound of footsteps echoed on the deck above. He took a deep breath, gripping the flare gun tightly. The cabin was small and cramped, and he could hear the intruder moving about, searching.

The footsteps grew louder, and Sam's heart pounded in his chest. He positioned himself behind the door, ready to confront the man the moment he stepped inside.

A Dangerous Encounter

The door swung open with a loud creak, and the intruder stepped inside, his face shadowed but menacing. Sam raised the flare gun, aiming it at the man's chest.

"Stop right there!" Sam shouted, his voice steady despite the adrenaline coursing through him.

The man froze, eyes widening as he registered the situation. "You think that little toy will stop me?" he sneered, reaching for something in his jacket.

"Don't move!" Sam warned, his finger hovering over the trigger.

"Go ahead, fire it," the man taunted, a twisted grin spreading across his face. "It won't save you."

With a sudden surge of anger, Sam squeezed the trigger. The flare shot out, illuminating the cabin in a bright, blinding light. The man staggered back, momentarily stunned by the flash.

Seizing the opportunity, Sam lunged forward, tackling the man to the ground. They tumbled across the floor, grappling for control. The man was strong, and Sam could feel his heart racing as he struggled to gain the upper hand.

"Lena!" Sam shouted, desperate for her to hear him. "Are you okay?"

"I'm fine!" she called from her hiding spot, but her voice was laced with anxiety.

The man managed to shove Sam off, scrambling to his feet. Sam quickly recovered, lunging forward again, but the man was ready this time. He swung a fist, catching Sam in the jaw and sending him sprawling against the cabin wall.

A Fight for Survival

Dazed but determined, Sam pushed himself up, shaking off the stars in his vision. He charged at the man once more, fueled by the need to protect Lena. They collided again, grappling for dominance in the confined space of the cabin.

"You have no idea what you're messing with!" the man spat, a hint of desperation creeping into his tone.

"I know you're a threat to Lena, and that's all I need to know," Sam replied, his voice fierce. With a sudden burst of strength, he slammed the man against the wall, pinning him there.

"Let me go!" the man shouted, struggling against Sam's hold.

"No way," Sam said, his muscles straining. "You're not getting away."

Just then, he heard the sound of a motor revving outside, and panic surged through him. They had only a moment before backup arrived.

"Lena!" Sam yelled. "Get ready to run!"

"Got it!" she shouted, emerging from her hiding spot, determination etched on her face.

In that moment of distraction, the man wrenched free, throwing Sam off balance. He lunged for the door, but Sam quickly recovered, blocking his path.

"You're not going anywhere," Sam growled, grabbing the man's arm.

With a sudden twist, the man managed to break free and barreled past Sam, heading for the exit. Sam chased after him, adrenaline fueling his every step.

The Chase Continues

As they burst onto the deck, the chaos of the night unfolded before them. The intruder sprinted towards the side of the yacht, clearly intent on making his escape. Sam's heart raced as he sprinted after him, the sound of the motor growing louder.

"Stop!" Sam yelled, desperation coloring his voice.

But the man was relentless, vaulting over the railing and into the water below. Sam hesitated for a split second, his mind racing. They had to act fast.

"Lena, we need to get the boat started now!" he shouted, urgency lacing his tone.

"I'm on it!" Lena replied, already rushing back inside the cabin.

As Sam watched the man swim away into the dark water, he realized they couldn't afford to lose any more time. He grabbed the small life raft from the side of the boat, hurling it into the water before jumping in after it.

Chapter 10: Sam's Psychological Insights Deepen

As the yacht drifted further from the chaotic scene of the attempted abduction, Sam found himself grappling with more than just the adrenaline from their escape. The night air was thick with the scent of saltwater and the distant sounds of the city, but his mind raced with thoughts that ran deeper than survival. They had narrowly escaped, but the encounter had unearthed feelings within him that he struggled to articulate, even to himself.

Lena had settled beside him in the dinghy, her face pale from the shock of their experience. The fear in her eyes haunted him, and he wanted nothing more than to reassure her. But the truth was, he was battling his own demons.

"Sam, are you okay?" Lena's voice broke through his thoughts, laced with concern.

He turned to her, forcing a smile despite the turmoil inside. "Yeah, I'm fine. Just... processing everything."

"Processing? It feels like we just barely escaped a nightmare!" She hugged her knees to her chest, her voice trembling.

"Exactly," he replied, his tone softening. "And that's what I need to think about. Why did they come after us? What do they want?"

Lena met his gaze, the fear in her eyes slowly shifting to curiosity. "Do you think it's connected to what happened with the murder?"

"It has to be," Sam said, his analytical mind already piecing together the fragments of their recent encounters. "But there's more. This feels personal. They were too focused on us. It's like they were hunting us down."

Lena shivered, and Sam instinctively moved closer, offering his warmth. "We'll figure it out together," he said firmly. "But we need to understand their motivations if we're going to protect ourselves."

Delving into the Mind

As the dinghy bobbed gently on the waves, Sam's thoughts spiraled deeper into the psychology of fear, control, and trauma. He had dedicated his life to understanding the human mind, and yet, in that moment, he found himself both a psychologist and a victim.

"The mind is a complicated labyrinth," he mused aloud, more to himself than to Lena. "In moments of crisis, we often revert to our most primal instincts: fight or flight."

Lena looked up, her interest piqued. "So you're saying they were acting on instinct?"

"Partly," Sam explained, his voice steadying as he fell into a familiar rhythm of analysis. "But there's also something deeper at play. People who resort to violence often have unresolved trauma or deep-seated fears that drive their behavior."

"Like a vicious cycle?" Lena asked, her eyes narrowing as she tried to comprehend.

"Exactly. They might be lashing out because they feel threatened or powerless in their own lives. It's a projection of their pain onto others. It's fascinating and tragic all at once," he said, feeling the weight of the subject.

Lena nodded slowly, absorbing his insights. "So you think they see us as a threat?"

"I think they see us as a target," Sam replied, the realization hitting him like a tidal wave. "We're linked to something they want to control or eliminate. Maybe it's about power."

"What do you mean?" Lena asked, her brow furrowed.

"Think about it," Sam continued, excitement creeping into his voice as he connected the dots. "Our investigation into the murder might have uncovered something they're desperate to keep hidden. They're willing to do whatever it takes to silence us."

Lena's eyes widened, the implications sinking in. "So it's not just a random attack? There's a purpose behind it?"

"Yes," Sam affirmed, feeling the pieces of the puzzle fall into place. "And that means we need to be even more careful. Understanding their motivations could be the key to staying one step ahead."

A Wave of Insight

As they drifted further from the yacht, the stars began to twinkle overhead, creating a serene contrast to the chaos they had just escaped. Sam took a deep breath, trying to find calm in the storm brewing within his mind.

"Lena, do you remember the first time we met?" he asked, his tone shifting to a more reflective one.

She tilted her head, the corners of her mouth lifting slightly. "Of course! You were that serious psychologist giving a talk on trauma. I was so nervous being in the same room as you."

"Right," Sam chuckled, remembering her nervous energy and the way she had fidgeted with her notes. "But I also remember how you challenged me during the Q&A. You had such a unique perspective on relationships and healing."

"Yeah, I was just trying to keep up with you," she said, a hint of pride in her voice. "But you really opened my eyes to the importance of understanding our past."

"That's what I love about psychology," Sam said, his passion igniting. "It's not just about understanding ourselves but understanding how our experiences shape our relationships with others. The more we understand ourselves, the better equipped we are to navigate the world."

Lena leaned back, looking up at the stars. "I think I'm starting to understand that more now. Everything we've been through has made me rethink my own past and how I relate to people."

"Exactly," Sam said, his voice earnest. "Trauma can create walls that keep us isolated. But if we can confront those walls and break them down, we can connect with others on a deeper level."

Confronting Their Own Walls

Lena shifted in her seat, her expression contemplative. "Do you think we're facing our walls right now?"

Sam paused, considering her words. "In a way, yes. We're both dealing with our fears and insecurities. The danger we're in amplifies those feelings, and we have to confront them head-on."

"I've spent so much time running from my past," Lena admitted, her voice barely above a whisper. "But I can't do that anymore. I want to face it, to understand why I've made the choices I have."

"That's a brave decision," Sam said, admiration swelling within him. "Facing our demons is never easy. But it's a crucial step toward healing and empowerment."

Lena turned to him, her eyes glistening. "What about you, Sam? Have you faced your demons?"

The question caught him off guard. Sam hesitated, reflecting on his own past—the guilt, the burden of expectations, and the need to save everyone he cared about. "I've tried," he finally admitted. "But I think I've avoided confronting some of my deeper fears. I have this nagging feeling that if I allow myself to feel vulnerable, I'll lose control."

"Control," Lena echoed softly, as if the word itself had weight. "It's a tricky thing. We crave it, yet it can isolate us from others."

"That's the paradox," Sam said, nodding in agreement. "In trying to maintain control, we often push people away or fail to connect with them authentically."

Finding Connection

The dinghy drifted quietly, the moonlight illuminating their faces as they continued to talk, opening up in ways that felt both exhilarating and terrifying.

"Do you ever feel like you're stuck in a loop?" Lena asked suddenly. "Like you keep replaying the same patterns in relationships?"

"Absolutely," Sam responded, feeling a connection to her words. "I've seen it in my clients, and I've experienced it myself. It's like we're drawn to the same scenarios, even when we know they're unhealthy."

"Exactly! It's frustrating," she said, her voice rising. "I want to break free from that cycle, but sometimes it feels impossible."

"It's not impossible," Sam reassured her, leaning closer. "It takes awareness and effort. And sometimes, it means being willing to confront the things we've buried deep."

Lena looked at him, a mixture of vulnerability and determination in her eyes. "I want to confront my past, Sam. I want to understand why I've made the choices I have, and how to break that cycle."

"That's a courageous decision," he said, feeling a swell of admiration for her. "And I want to help you through it. You don't have to do it alone."

"Thank you," she whispered, her voice trembling. "It means so much to have you by my side."

In that moment, under the stars, they both felt the weight of their fears and insecurities lift, if only slightly. It was a moment of clarity amidst the chaos, a shared understanding that their journey wasn't just about survival—it was about healing and connection.

A Shared Purpose

As the waves gently rocked the dinghy, Sam and Lena sat in silence, contemplating the road ahead. The danger they faced had brought them closer, but it was the understanding they were forging that would ultimately guide them through the darkness.

"I've always believed that understanding our trauma can lead to healing," Sam said finally, his voice steady. "But I also know that it can be painful. Are you prepared for that?"

Lena took a deep breath, her expression resolute. "I am. I've spent too long hiding from it. I want to confront it all—my past, my choices, everything."

"Good," Sam said, his heart swelling with pride. "And I'll be here every step of the way. But remember, it's not just about facing the darkness. It's also about recognizing the light that comes from it."

Lena nodded, a small smile forming on her lips. "I'll hold onto that."

"Let's promise each other something," Sam said, his tone serious. "No matter what happens next, we'll communicate openly."

Chapter 11: Building Trust Between Sam and Lena

As dawn broke over the horizon, the first rays of sunlight danced upon the water, casting a golden hue over the dinghy. Sam and Lena sat quietly, wrapped in a comforting silence that felt almost sacred after the chaos of the night before. The world felt renewed in the soft morning light, a stark contrast to the fear that had gripped them just hours earlier.

"Do you think they're still looking for us?" Lena broke the silence, her voice still hoarse from the night's adrenaline.

"I wouldn't doubt it," Sam replied, scanning the horizon for any signs of danger. "But for now, we have a little time to breathe and regroup. Our priority is to get to safety and figure out our next move."

Lena nodded, her brow furrowed in thought. "And to piece together what's really going on. I can't shake the feeling that everything is connected—the murder, the men from last night, and my past."

"You're right," Sam said, turning to face her. "It's all part of a larger puzzle. But we need to be strategic. Let's focus on building trust between us while we navigate this."

Lena looked at him, the vulnerability of the previous night lingering in her gaze. "Trust... that's a big word, Sam. Especially considering what we've been through."

"I know," he replied, his tone gentle but firm. "But trust is essential, especially in situations like this. We need to rely on each other if we're going to uncover the truth and keep ourselves safe."

The Foundation of Trust

They spent the next few moments discussing what trust meant to each of them. For Sam, it was about honesty and transparency, knowing that vulnerability was not a weakness but a strength. For Lena, trust was intertwined with her past experiences—something she had struggled with since her childhood.

"I've been let down so many times," she confessed, her voice soft but steady. "It's hard for me to open up fully. I've learned to keep my guard up."

"I understand that," Sam said, feeling a pang of empathy. "But we can't let past experiences dictate our present. This is a new chapter for both of us, and it requires a leap of faith."

"What if I don't know how to take that leap?" Lena asked, her eyes reflecting her uncertainty.

"Then let's take it together," Sam proposed, a spark of determination igniting within him. "We can start with small steps—sharing more about ourselves, being honest about our feelings, and communicating openly about our fears and hopes."

Lena contemplated his words, her expression thoughtful. "That sounds... doable. But I'll need your help to break down those walls. It's not something I can do alone."

"Absolutely," he assured her, feeling a warmth spread in his chest. "I'm here for you, every step of the way."

Shared Vulnerabilities

The morning sun rose higher, casting a gentle warmth over them as they drifted further into open waters. Sam decided to share a piece of his past, hoping it would encourage Lena to do the same.

"When I was in college, I struggled with trusting people," he began, his voice steady. "I lost a close friend to suicide. It shattered my world and made me question everything I thought I knew about connection."

Lena's gaze softened, and she leaned in, her curiosity piqued. "What happened?"

"I had always believed I could help people—be the savior, you know? But in that moment, I realized I wasn't enough. I had pushed him away, thinking I could fix him without fully understanding his pain. It took me years to realize that sometimes, just being there for someone is more powerful than trying to save them."

Lena listened intently, her expression shifting from curiosity to empathy. "That's incredibly brave of you to share, Sam. I can't imagine how difficult that was."

"It was," he admitted, the memories flooding back. "But it taught me the importance of connection. I realized that trust is built through vulnerability, even when it scares us. It's okay to be imperfect."

"Thank you for sharing that," Lena said, her voice thick with emotion. "It helps to know I'm not alone in this."

"You're not alone," Sam assured her, feeling a sense of connection solidifying between them. "Now it's your turn. Share something with me. What's been your biggest challenge in trusting others?"

Lena took a deep breath, her eyes reflecting a mixture of fear and determination. "My parents' divorce changed everything for me. I was just a kid, but I felt like I had to choose sides. I ended up shutting myself off emotionally because I didn't want to get hurt again."

"I can see how that would impact your ability to trust," Sam said gently. "Divorce can create a lot of emotional turmoil, especially for children."

"Exactly," Lena said, her voice trembling. "I thought if I didn't get close to anyone, I wouldn't have to deal with the pain of losing them. But now, I realize that it's been holding me back from truly living."

Creating a Safe Space

Sam nodded, feeling the weight of her words. "You're already taking a brave step by recognizing that. And you don't have to face this alone anymore. We can work through it together."

"Thank you," Lena replied, her voice softening. "That means more than you know. I want to trust you, Sam. I really do."

"Then let's keep building that trust, one conversation at a time," he encouraged, feeling the bond between them strengthen. "Let's make this our safe space. We can share our fears, our hopes, and everything in between."

As the sun climbed higher, illuminating the ocean in a dazzling array of colors, Sam and Lena felt a shift in their dynamic. The vulnerability they had shared created a foundation of trust—one that would support them as they ventured deeper into the mystery that lay ahead.

Developing a Strategy

As they settled into their new routine, they began to formulate a plan. Sam suggested they focus on gathering information about the murder and the people who had attacked them. They needed to dig deeper into Lena's past and uncover any potential links to the present.

"We should start by looking into your life before the gala," Sam suggested. "Were there any connections to people who might have known about your past?"

Lena furrowed her brow, deep in thought. "I'll have to think about it. There are certain people I've kept at a distance because of my childhood experiences. Maybe they could shed light on what's happening."

"Great," Sam replied, feeling encouraged. "The more we know, the better equipped we'll be to handle whatever comes next."

They began to brainstorm, making a list of people Lena could reach out to. Friends from her childhood, acquaintances from work, even her therapist. The goal was to gather as much information as possible, but also to confront her past.

"I want to understand why I've been running," Lena said, determination etched in her voice. "I need to face it head-on."

Sam smiled, feeling a swell of pride for her bravery. "That's the spirit. And remember, I'm here to support you through this."

The Journey of Trust

As the day wore on, the sun began to dip towards the horizon, painting the sky in shades of orange and purple. They continued to talk and strategize, the connection between them deepening with each shared vulnerability.

"Do you think trust can ever be fully restored once it's broken?" Lena asked, her voice reflective.

Sam pondered the question, considering his own experiences. "I believe it can, but it takes time, effort, and a commitment to honesty. It requires both parties to be willing to confront their feelings and communicate openly."

"I want to get there," Lena said, her voice steady. "I want to be able to trust again—not just you, but myself too."

"That's a powerful intention," Sam said, feeling a warmth spread through him. "It's about recognizing that trust is not just about the other person—it's also about trusting yourself to make the right choices."

Lena smiled, the weight of her fears beginning to lift. "I'm starting to see that. Maybe I can trust myself to lean into this process with you."

"Exactly," Sam said, feeling a sense of hope bloom within him. "And it's okay to take it one step at a time. We don't have to have all the answers right now."

"Just being here with you helps," Lena admitted, her eyes shining with gratitude. "I can feel the trust building between us, and it feels... freeing."

"Good," Sam replied, his heart swelling with warmth. "That's what this is all about—creating a safe space where we can be vulnerable and honest."

Facing the Future Together

As they continued to navigate the open waters, Sam felt a sense of clarity wash over him. Their journey together had become more than just a fight for survival; it was about understanding themselves and each other on a deeper level.

"We'll face whatever comes next together," Sam said, his voice firm. "And we'll do it with honesty and trust."

Lena nodded, her expression resolute. "I'm ready, Sam. Let's confront this together."

As they drifted into the evening, the stars began to twinkle above them, a reminder of the vastness of the universe and the journey that lay ahead. Sam and Lena sat side by side, the bond between them growing stronger with each passing moment. They were no longer just a psychologist and a client—they were partners, united in their quest for truth, healing, and connection.

And as the night enveloped them, they knew they would face the darkness.

Chapter 12: The Revelation

The following days drifted by in a whirlwind of tense moments and whispered conversations as Sam and Lena navigated their new reality. With each passing hour, their connection deepened, fueled by trust and shared vulnerability. Yet, the shadow of danger loomed ever closer, and the mystery surrounding Lena's past and the murder began to unfold like a tightly woven tapestry, slowly revealing its secrets.

Sam had been compiling information on the murder victim, an influential socialite named Celeste Harper, whose untimely death had sent shockwaves through the elite circles of the city. The investigation had hit a dead end, but Sam felt a growing urgency to connect the dots, especially given the strange occurrences surrounding Lena.

On a particularly overcast afternoon, they found themselves back on the yacht. The calm waters were deceptive, masking the storm of emotions brewing beneath the surface. Sam had arranged for them to stay aboard while he continued his investigation, and the sense of security the yacht provided allowed Lena to breathe a little easier.

"Do you think we're getting closer to the truth?" Lena asked, her voice tinged with anxiety as she leaned against the railing, staring out at the horizon.

"I do," Sam replied, his mind racing with the latest pieces of information. "But we need to dig deeper into Celeste's life. She had a reputation that suggests she wasn't just a socialite. There's something more to her story, and I think it ties back to you."

Lena turned to him, her brows furrowing in concern. "How could I possibly be connected to someone like her?"

"From what I've gathered, Celeste was involved in some shady dealings, especially regarding her wealth and connections. You mentioned knowing some of the same people in the industry. Have you ever had any encounters with her?" Sam pressed, eager to piece together the puzzle.

Lena hesitated, her face clouded with uncertainty. "I remember hearing her name in conversations, but I never met her directly. My circles were more modest. Still, I did attend a charity gala once where she was the guest of honor. That's about it."

Sam nodded, taking mental notes. "A starting point, nonetheless. We should see if there are any connections that link you to her, however tenuous. It might give us a better understanding of why you're being targeted."

Lena nodded, the weight of their task settling heavily on her shoulders. "Okay, I'll try to remember anything I can. But what if there's more to this than just a connection to Celeste? What if it's about something I did?"

"Let's not jump to conclusions," Sam reassured her, placing a gentle hand on her arm. "Focus on what you do remember. The truth often reveals itself in unexpected ways."

A Trail of Clues

Over the next few days, they meticulously combed through records, social media, and news articles related to Celeste Harper. Each detail seemed to deepen the mystery, yet none provided concrete evidence to connect Lena to the murder. The tension in the air was palpable as they both felt the weight of their pursuit.

One evening, as they sat on the deck, the sun setting in a fiery orange glow, Lena turned to Sam with a determined look. "What if we reached out to some of the people I know from that gala? Maybe someone has insights into Celeste's life or death. It's worth a shot."

Sam considered her suggestion. "That's a great idea. But let's approach it carefully. We don't want to raise any suspicions. We can contact them casually, as if we're just trying to learn more about the event."

"Right," Lena agreed, her voice gaining confidence. "I can start with a couple of friends who might have known her better. They might have been closer to her circle."

"Let's do it," Sam encouraged, feeling a spark of hope ignite within him. "And in the meantime, I'll continue to dig into Celeste's background. I have a few contacts I can reach out to."

A Break in the Case

As they worked together, Lena's memories began to resurface. She recalled snippets of conversations from the gala, whispers of rivalries, jealousy, and secrets swirling around Celeste. One name kept coming up—Vivian Sinclair, a socialite known for her sharp wit and even sharper tongue.

"Vivian was Celeste's closest friend," Lena said, her brow furrowing in concentration. "They were practically inseparable, but I heard they had a falling out not long before Celeste's death."

"That's interesting," Sam replied, jotting down the name. "Do you remember why they fell out?"

"Something about a business deal gone wrong," Lena said slowly. "I think Celeste invested in something that didn't pan out, and Vivian was furious. It caused quite a stir in their circles."

"That could be a significant lead," Sam noted, his excitement building. "If they were close, it might explain some of the animosity surrounding her death. We should find out more about Vivian's whereabouts during the murder."

Lena nodded, her eyes shining with determination. "I can reach out to a friend who might have insights into Vivian. She's been around that scene long enough to know if there's more to the story."

The Web Unravels

A couple of days later, Lena received a message from her friend, Sarah, who had insights into Vivian Sinclair's movements around the time of the murder. Lena shared the details with Sam as they sat on the deck, the atmosphere charged with anticipation.

"Sarah said that Vivian was in town for a charity event the night Celeste was murdered, but she left early," Lena explained, her brow creasing with worry. "There are whispers that she and Celeste had a heated argument the week before."

"Sounds like there might be more to this than just a simple falling out," Sam remarked, piecing together the puzzle. "What if Vivian had a motive?"

"Or maybe she was being manipulated by someone else," Lena suggested. "Celeste had many enemies, and jealousy can drive people to extremes."

"Let's see if we can track down Vivian," Sam said, his determination solidifying. "We need to confront her and see if she knows anything about Celeste's death—and your connection to it."

They spent the next few hours devising a plan to reach out to Vivian. Sam crafted a message, subtly hinting at their shared connections while keeping their true intentions hidden. Lena sent it off, her heart racing at the thought of potentially unearthing more secrets.

The Meeting

The following evening, a response came in from Vivian. She agreed to meet them at a nearby café, a choice that struck Sam as both fortuitous and risky. They had no idea what they might be walking into, but they were determined to confront the truth.

"Are you ready for this?" Sam asked Lena as they prepared to leave the yacht, tension radiating from her.

"As ready as I'll ever be," she replied, her voice steady yet laced with apprehension. "I need to know the truth, even if it's painful."

"Exactly," Sam encouraged, sensing her resolve. "Just remember to stay focused. We're here to gather information, not to get pulled into any emotional traps."

Lena nodded, her expression shifting from uncertainty to determination. "Let's do this."

A Face-to-Face Encounter

The café was bustling with life as they entered, the aroma of fresh coffee and baked goods wrapping around them like a warm embrace. They spotted Vivian sitting at a corner table, her presence commanding attention even amidst the chaos. Her sharp features and confident demeanor exuded an air of elegance, but there was an underlying tension in her gaze as she noticed them approaching.

"Lena, darling! What a surprise to see you here," Vivian exclaimed, her voice dripping with a mix of charm and wariness.

"Thank you for meeting with us," Lena said, trying to keep her voice steady as she sat down across from her.

"Of course," Vivian replied, her eyes narrowing slightly as she regarded Sam. "And who's your friend?"

"This is Dr. Sam Cross, a psychologist," Lena introduced, sensing the tension in the air. "He's been helping me navigate some... personal issues."

Vivian's expression shifted, curiosity mingling with skepticism. "Interesting. What brings you two to me?"

"We wanted to talk about Celeste Harper," Sam said, his voice calm and steady. "We've been looking into her murder, and we believe you may have valuable insights."

Vivian's demeanor changed in an instant, the facade of charm slipping away to reveal something more guarded. "Celeste? What could I possibly know that you don't?"

"We've heard about your close friendship," Sam pressed gently, watching for any signs of discomfort. "And the falling out that occurred before her death."

Vivian leaned back in her chair, crossing her arms defensively. "That's ancient history. Everyone has arguments. It doesn't mean I killed her."

"Not at all," Lena interjected, feeling the tension thickening the air. "But we think it's important to understand what happened between you two. You were the last person to see her, right?"

Vivian's gaze flickered for a moment, a hint of something darker lurking beneath her composed exterior. "I was, but that doesn't mean I was involved in her death. Our disagreement was personal, nothing more."

"Was it about a business deal?" Sam inquired, keenly observing her reactions.

"Something like that," Vivian replied, her tone dismissive. "Celeste was reckless with her investments. I tried to warn her, but she wouldn't listen."

"Did she ever mention feeling threatened by anyone?" Lena pressed, feeling the urgency in her heart.

Chapter 13: Confrontation with the Antagonist

The air in the café thickened as Lena and Sam sat across from Vivian Sinclair, tension palpable between them. The lingering whispers of suspicion hovered in the space like a dark cloud, and Lena could feel her heart racing. The time had come to peel back the layers of deception surrounding Celeste Harper's murder, and Vivian was at the center of it all.

"Did Celeste mention feeling threatened by anyone?" Lena pressed again, her voice steady despite the turmoil swirling inside her.

Vivian's expression tightened, and she leaned forward slightly. "You're digging too deep, dear. Celeste had her fair share of enemies, but who doesn't in this world? She was a powerful woman with powerful connections. That comes with its own set of dangers."

"Were you one of those dangers?" Sam asked, his tone sharp. "You mentioned a falling out. What did you mean by that?"

Vivian's eyes narrowed, and for a moment, the mask of elegance slipped, revealing a flash of anger. "It was a disagreement over business, nothing more. Celeste had a tendency to get herself into situations she couldn't handle. I tried to protect her, but she refused to listen."

"Protect her or sabotage her?" Sam countered, his gaze unwavering. "What was it that you stood to gain?"

Vivian let out a cold laugh, her demeanor shifting to one of disdain. "You think I'm capable of murder? You don't know the half of it.

Celeste was reckless, but I never wished her dead. I may have wanted her out of my way, but not like that."

"Tell us about the last time you saw her," Lena urged, desperation creeping into her voice. "It could help us understand your relationship better."

Vivian sighed, as if weighing her options. "Fine. The last time I saw Celeste was at a gala. We had an argument—one of many—and she stormed off. I left shortly after, but I didn't think anything of it."

"And you have no idea what happened to her after that?" Sam pressed.

"None," Vivian snapped, her frustration evident. "I left and went home. What happened afterward is beyond my control."

Lena exchanged a glance with Sam, sensing the tension escalating. "But you knew something was wrong," Lena said, her tone softening. "Why would you agree to meet us today if you had nothing to hide?"

Vivian's gaze darted around the café, as if searching for an escape. "Because I'm tired of being accused. I want to clear my name. Celeste was complicated, and our relationship was... volatile. But that doesn't mean I killed her."

"Then help us," Sam urged. "If you truly want to clear your name, share everything you know. We're not your enemies here."

Vivian seemed to wrestle with her thoughts, her facade beginning to crack. "Fine. There's something I didn't mention. Celeste had been meeting with some shady characters. I don't know the details, but I had a bad feeling about it. I warned her to stay away from them, but she didn't listen."

"Who were they?" Lena asked, leaning in closer.

"I don't know their names. Just that they were involved in something illegal. I overheard her on the phone once, speaking in hushed tones," Vivian confessed, her voice trembling slightly. "She was in deep, and I couldn't pull her out."

"What if those connections are linked to her murder?" Sam suggested. "That might explain why you're being targeted too."

Vivian's expression hardened, and she seemed to regain her composure. "Look, I may not have liked Celeste, but I didn't want her dead. I just wanted her to stop being so reckless."

Lena felt a pang of sympathy for Vivian, realizing that beneath her cold exterior lay a complex web of emotions. "If that's true, then we need to work together. This isn't just about you anymore. It's about finding the truth."

Vivian's gaze softened for a moment, revealing a flicker of vulnerability. "You have no idea how dangerous this can get. If those men Celeste was dealing with find out that we're investigating..."

"Then we'll protect each other," Sam assured her, his tone serious. "But we need your help to figure this out."

Vivian hesitated, weighing her options. "Alright. I'll help you. But know this—I want no part in whatever mess this is. I've got my own life to live."

"Then let's start by finding out who Celeste was involved with," Lena said, feeling a surge of determination.

A Dangerous Connection

As the conversation continued, Lena felt the weight of the mystery deepening. Vivian shared what little she knew about Celeste's dealings, hinting at connections with powerful figures who operated in the shadows. It became clear that they were delving into a world filled with danger and deception.

"We need to dig into Celeste's contacts," Sam suggested, taking charge of the situation. "If she was involved with these shady characters, there might be a paper trail we can follow."

Vivian nodded reluctantly. "I can help with that. I have contacts in the social scene who might know something."

"Let's do it," Lena urged, her heart racing at the thought of uncovering more layers to the mystery. "But we need to be careful. This could lead us into a trap."

"I'll arrange a meeting with one of Celeste's acquaintances," Vivian said, her demeanor shifting to one of determination. "But if this gets dangerous, I'm out. I won't risk my life for her mistakes."

"Fair enough," Sam agreed, understanding the stakes. "We'll approach this cautiously."

Setting the Trap

The next few days were filled with frantic planning and preparations. Lena, Sam, and Vivian worked closely to gather information, following leads that seemed to stretch into the depths of a hidden underworld. The tension in the air was thick, each new revelation pushing them further down a path filled with uncertainty.

Finally, they secured a meeting with one of Celeste's associates—a man named Derek Holloway, known for his connections in both the social and business worlds. Vivian insisted on being present, eager to assert her involvement in the investigation.

As they approached the upscale restaurant where the meeting was scheduled, Lena could feel her heart pounding. "This could be it," she whispered to Sam, anxiety creeping into her voice.

"Stay focused," Sam replied, squeezing her hand reassuringly. "We're here for answers. Remember what we discussed—stick to the plan."

The trio entered the restaurant, the ambiance buzzing with life and chatter. They spotted Derek at a corner table, his presence commanding attention even amidst the crowd. He was impeccably dressed, exuding an air of confidence and charm, but Lena sensed an underlying menace lurking beneath his polished exterior.

"Derek, thanks for meeting us," Vivian greeted him, her voice dripping with a mix of familiarity and apprehension. "I hope we're not imposing."

"Not at all," Derek replied, his gaze flickering over Lena and Sam. "I hear you're looking for information on Celeste. Quite the mystery, isn't it?"

"Indeed," Sam interjected smoothly, taking the lead. "We have some questions about her recent activities. We believe they may be connected to her murder."

Derek raised an eyebrow, his amusement barely concealed. "Murder, you say? That's quite a serious accusation."

"We're just trying to piece together what happened," Lena added, trying to remain composed. "What can you tell us about Celeste's recent dealings?"

Derek leaned back in his chair, a calculating look in his eyes. "Celeste was a woman of many talents. She had her hands in various pots, but she often overstepped her boundaries. People like us—" he gestured around the restaurant, "—we know how to play the game. Celeste was more reckless."

"Reckless how?" Sam pressed, sensing a hint of evasion.

"She dabbled in investments that were... less than reputable," Derek explained, a smirk playing on his lips. "And she didn't care who she stepped on to get what she wanted."

"Did you know anyone who might have wanted to harm her?" Lena asked, her heart racing as she sensed the tension escalating.

"Potentially," Derek replied, his tone shifting slightly. "But I'm not in the habit of keeping tabs on everyone. The world can be a dangerous place when you're involved with the wrong people."

"Do you know who those 'wrong people' are?" Sam pressed.

Derek's expression darkened, a flicker of warning flashing in his eyes. "Let's not get too deep into this, shall we? Some things are better left untouched."

Lena felt a surge of frustration but remained calm. "We need the truth, Derek. If there's anything you know that can help us, now is the time to speak up."

"Watch your tone, sweetheart," he snapped, his demeanor shifting dangerously. "You're treading into waters you don't understand."

The Confrontation Escalates

In that moment, Lena felt the tension snap like a taut string. Derek's charm had melted away, revealing the true threat he posed. "You think you can intimidate us?" Sam challenged, his voice steady. "We're not afraid of you or your threats."

Derek's eyes glinted with menace. "You don't know who you're dealing with. This isn't just about Celeste anymore. You've crossed a line, and there are consequences for that."

"Consequences? You think you can silence us?" Lena's voice trembled with determination. "We're not going to back down".

Chapter 14: Emotional Struggles

The adrenaline of the confrontation with Derek Holloway had barely begun to fade when Lena, Sam, and Vivian left the upscale restaurant, the heavy weight of dread settling over them like a storm cloud. The encounter had escalated quickly, and the implications of their pursuit of the truth were beginning to feel dangerously real.

"Do you think he'll come after us?" Lena asked, her voice a mixture of fear and uncertainty as they stepped out into the cool evening air.

Vivian's face was pale, her confidence from earlier replaced with a flicker of anxiety. "He's not the type to take threats lightly. We need to be cautious."

"I don't care what he thinks," Sam declared, his jaw set with determination. "We're not backing down now. We're closer than ever to understanding what happened to Celeste."

"But at what cost?" Lena replied, her brow furrowed as she struggled to keep her emotions in check. "We just confronted someone dangerous, and we still don't know who else is involved."

"We'll handle it together," Sam reassured her, taking her hand in his, grounding her in the moment. "But we need to take immediate precautions. Let's lay low for a while, regroup, and figure out our next steps."

As they walked back to the yacht, the world around them felt surreal. The bustling city streets, illuminated by neon lights and vibrant energy, seemed to mock the turmoil brewing within them. Lena felt as though she were caught in a whirlwind, her heart racing with fear and excitement, yet it all felt overshadowed by a growing sense of dread.

Inside the Yacht

Once aboard the yacht, the weight of the confrontation settled heavily upon them. Lena sank into a plush chair in the small living area, her mind racing. "I can't believe we just confronted him. What if he comes after us? What if he knows where we are?"

"Then we'll be ready," Sam said, his tone steady as he moved closer to her. "We'll get security measures in place. I have contacts who can help."

"Sam, this isn't just about security measures," she replied, her voice rising with emotion. "This is about my life—about everything that's happened to me. I don't want to live in fear anymore."

"I understand," he said softly, crouching beside her, searching her eyes. "But we have to keep going. We can't let them win."

Lena's heart ached at the weight of his words. "What if I can't keep going? I'm so tired of fighting."

"We're fighting for the truth," Sam insisted, his gaze unwavering. "And for you. I won't let anything happen to you, Lena. You're not alone in this."

His sincerity touched her deeply, yet her mind was clouded with uncertainty. The chaos of the past few weeks had taken its toll on her emotionally. She had lost herself in the investigation, but now, with the confrontation with Derek, she felt the emotional aftermath crashing over her like a tidal wave.

"I don't know how to handle this," Lena admitted, her voice barely above a whisper as tears threatened to spill over. "I've spent so long trying to be strong, but it feels like I'm just getting pulled further down."

Sam wrapped his arms around her, holding her tightly as she let the tears fall. "It's okay to feel this way. You're allowed to feel overwhelmed. Just know that I'm here for you."

In that moment, Lena felt the warmth of his embrace envelop her, a stark contrast to the cold reality outside. But beneath the comfort, she grappled with her past, with the traumas that had shaped her life and the choices she had made in the pursuit of survival.

Vivian's Struggle

Meanwhile, Vivian stood at the edge of the deck, staring out at the water as it glimmered under the moonlight. The confrontation had shaken her, too. She had always been the strong one, the one who manipulated situations to her advantage, but this had left her feeling vulnerable.

"Vivian?" Sam's voice pulled her from her thoughts, and she turned to face him. "Are you okay?"

"Just thinking," she replied, her voice steady despite the turmoil within. "That was intense, and I didn't expect it to escalate so quickly. I've been in some rough situations, but this... this is different."

"You can talk to us," Sam said gently, his concern evident. "We're in this together."

Vivian forced a smile, but it didn't reach her eyes. "I appreciate that, but I've been on my own for so long. It's hard to open up."

Lena joined them, wiping her tears as she walked over to Vivian. "You don't have to go through this alone. We need each other right now more than ever."

Vivian looked between them, her guarded expression softening slightly. "I guess I'm just scared of what this means for all of us. I've had my fair share of enemies, but I never thought I'd be dragged into a murder investigation."

"You're not alone in this," Lena reassured her. "We'll face whatever comes together."

Vivian nodded slowly, taking a deep breath. "Alright. Let's figure this out. I have some contacts who can help us dig deeper into Celeste's past. We need to find out who she was involved with and why she was in danger."

"Good idea," Sam agreed. "Let's make a plan. But first, we all need some rest. We can't fight this battle if we're running on empty."

As the trio settled into a tentative camaraderie, each held their own emotional struggles close. The bonds they were forming were fragile, yet they began to understand that they needed one another more than ever to navigate the storm ahead.

Reflections in the Night

Later that night, Lena found herself unable to sleep, her mind racing with thoughts. She stepped out onto the deck, the cool night air refreshing against her skin. The stars twinkled above, a million distant lights illuminating her path as she breathed deeply, trying to calm her racing heart.

"Can't sleep?" Sam's voice broke through the silence, and she turned to see him approaching.

"No," she admitted, her voice barely above a whisper. "I keep thinking about everything—Celeste, Derek, my past... it's all so overwhelming."

Sam stepped closer, the warmth of his presence soothing her nerves. "I know it feels like a lot, but you're not alone. You've got me, and I'm not going anywhere."

"Do you ever feel scared?" she asked, her vulnerability surfacing as she looked into his eyes. "I mean, really scared?"

"Every day," he confessed, his honesty surprising her. "But I've learned that fear can either paralyze you or push you to act. It's okay to feel scared, Lena. It means you're human."

"Sometimes, I wonder if I'm strong enough for all this," she admitted, her voice trembling. "I've faced so many challenges, but this feels different. I don't want to lose myself in it."

"You won't lose yourself," Sam reassured her, taking her hand gently. "We're fighting for you. You're stronger than you realize, and you have the power to break free from your past."

As they stood together under the vast night sky, Lena felt a flicker of hope ignite within her. Perhaps she didn't have to bear the weight of her struggles alone. The bond she shared with Sam and Vivian was beginning to form a lifeline, a connection that could guide her through the darkness.

Facing the Past

The following day, the trio gathered to devise a plan. Sam had contacted a few trusted associates who could help them dig deeper into Celeste's connections, while Vivian prepared to reach out to her social circle for information.

"We need to be methodical about this," Sam said, his demeanor shifting to that of a determined leader. "Let's break down our tasks. Vivian, you'll handle the social connections. Lena and I will focus on digging through Celeste's financial records and any dealings she might have had."

"Sounds good," Vivian agreed, her confidence returning. "I can make some calls and set up meetings with a few people who might know more about her recent activities."

Lena nodded, feeling a renewed sense of purpose. "Let's see if we can find any links to the shady characters Derek mentioned. It might lead us to the answers we're looking for."

As they delved into their tasks, Lena felt a sense of camaraderie blossoming between them. Each of them was driven by their own motivations, yet they were united by the common goal of uncovering the truth. With each piece of information they uncovered, they were drawing closer to the heart of the mystery.

The Toll of the Investigation

Days turned into nights as they worked tirelessly to piece together Celeste's life. The process was exhausting, each new revelation peeling back layers of deception and danger. But the emotional toll was beginning to weigh heavily on Lena.

She found herself drawn back into memories she had long tried to bury. The trauma of her past, the struggles she had faced, and the pain of loss surged to the surface, threatening to overwhelm her once again.

One evening, after a long day of investigating, Lena retreated to her room, the walls feeling like they were closing in on her. She sat on the edge of her bed, staring at the floor, tears pooling in her eyes.

"Lena?" Sam knocked gently on the door before entering, concern etched on his face. "Are you alright?"

"Not really," she admitted, her voice shaking. "I feel like I'm drowning in all of this."

Chapter 15: Healing Begins for Lena and Sam

The Aftermath of the Investigation

The weight of the past weeks still lingered in the air, even as the investigation into Celeste's murder was drawing to a close. Sam and Lena, though closer to the truth, had both come to realize that the journey had taken a heavy emotional toll on them. They had been so focused on the mystery, on uncovering what had happened to Celeste, that they hadn't fully confronted their own wounds.

Lena, standing on the deck of the yacht, gazed out at the water, the gentle rocking of the waves providing a fleeting sense of calm. She had felt broken before, but now there was something different—an opening. The experiences she had shared with Sam had cracked open parts of her that she had long buried.

"You're lost in thought again," Sam's voice came from behind her, soft and familiar.

Lena didn't turn to face him immediately, choosing instead to continue staring at the water. "It's hard not to be. So much has happened."

Sam walked over, leaning against the railing beside her. "You've been carrying a lot for a long time, Lena. It's okay to let go."

The words hit her hard, as if he had verbalized the very thing she feared: letting go. Letting go of the fear, the guilt, and the trauma that had defined her for so long. She had built walls around herself, but here, with Sam, those walls had begun to crumble.

"Do you ever wonder if healing is even possible?" she asked, her voice soft but laced with doubt.

"I think it's always possible," Sam said, his gaze steady on her. "But it's not something that happens all at once. It's small moments, small choices. And sometimes, it's allowing yourself to feel everything—without trying to fix it right away."

Lena turned to face him, her heart aching but hopeful. "I don't know if I'm ready to feel everything."

Own Journey

What Lena didn't know was that Sam, too, had his own healing to do. His role as a psychologist meant he was used to being the one to help others through their pain, but rarely did he confront his own. He had spent years analyzing trauma, delving into the minds of others, yet his own vulnerabilities often remained hidden behind the facade of professional competence.

"You've always been the strong one," Lena continued, breaking Sam's train of thought. "But I know there's more going on underneath."

Sam exhaled slowly, knowing this was a moment of truth. "I've spent a long time thinking that helping others would be enough. That by fixing the broken pieces in other people's lives, I could avoid looking at my own cracks. But you... you've made me see things differently."

"What do you mean?" Lena asked, genuinely curious.

"You've reminded me that I can't run from my own pain," he admitted, his voice thick with emotion. "I've lost people, too. I've faced my own trauma, but I've always buried it in work. With you, I can't hide anymore. You make me want to be better, for both of us."

For a long moment, they stood in silence, the shared weight of their individual pain filling the space between them. But unlike before, there was no suffocating tension—only an unspoken understanding that they had to confront these emotions to move forward.

The First Steps Toward Healing

That night, Sam and Lena decided to take their first steps toward true healing. They both knew that it wouldn't be easy, that there were years of wounds, trust issues, and traumas to unpack. But in each other, they found a safe space, a refuge from the chaos.

Lena sat down at the small kitchen table on the yacht, pulling out an old journal she hadn't touched in years. Writing had always been her way of coping, but for so long, she had been too scared to confront the past.

"I used to write to make sense of things," she said quietly, her fingers brushing the worn pages. "But I stopped when things got too dark. I didn't want to remember anymore."

Sam sat across from her, his eyes soft with understanding. "You don't have to share it with me if you're not ready."

"No, I want to," Lena replied, surprising herself with the words. "I think I need to. Maybe talking about it will help."

For the next hour, Lena slowly began to read passages from her journal aloud. The entries were raw and filled with the anguish she had experienced—abuse, betrayal, loneliness. As she read, tears streamed down her face, but she didn't stop. Sam sat quietly, listening, offering her his silent support.

When she finished, Lena wiped her eyes and let out a shaky breath. "I've never read that out loud before."

"You're incredibly brave," Sam said, his voice full of awe. "I know that wasn't easy."

"It wasn't," she admitted. "But I feel... lighter. Like I don't have to hold it all in anymore."

"That's the first step," Sam said, smiling gently. "And I'll be here for every step after this."

Trust and Vulnerability

As the days passed, Sam and Lena found themselves leaning on one another more than ever before. It wasn't just about solving Celeste's murder anymore; it was about rediscovering who they were beneath the masks they had worn for so long.

One afternoon, while the sun bathed the yacht in golden light, Sam approached Lena with something he had been meaning to share.

"I think it's time I tell you about my past," Sam said quietly, sitting down beside her.

Lena looked at him curiously, sensing the gravity in his tone. "You don't have to—"

"No, I want to," Sam interrupted gently. "You've shared so much with me. It's only fair that I open up, too."

For the first time, Sam revealed the depth of his own struggles—his strained relationship with his father, the loss of a close friend during his early career, and the pressure he had always felt to be the "fixer" in everyone's life.

"I guess I've always felt responsible for everyone else's happiness," Sam admitted, his voice tinged with sadness. "But somewhere along the way, I forgot about my own."

"You don't have to carry that burden alone anymore," Lena whispered, reaching for his hand. "We're in this together now."

Sam smiled, a warmth spreading through him. "I never thought I'd find someone who could understand me like this. You make me feel like it's okay to be vulnerable."

"It is," Lena said softly. "You've taught me that."

Finding a New Path Together

As weeks passed, Lena and Sam began to build a new rhythm, one that wasn't dominated by the investigation or their past traumas. They made time for quiet moments—long walks along the shore, dinners where they laughed and forgot the world, and nights spent wrapped in each other's arms, simply being.

They weren't healed completely; both knew that healing was a lifelong journey. But they were on the path, and for the first time in a long time, it felt like they weren't walking it alone.

One evening, as they sat on the deck watching the sun set, Sam turned to Lena with a question that had been on his mind. "Do you ever think about the future? What comes next, after all of this?"

Lena smiled, a genuine smile that reflected the hope she hadn't felt in a long time. "I do. And for the first time, I think I'm ready for it."

"Me too," Sam said softly, taking her hand. "Whatever it is, we'll face it together."

As the sun dipped below the horizon, casting the sky in hues of orange and pink, Lena and Sam sat in silence, content in the knowledge that they were healing, slowly but surely. They had been through the storm, but now, they were beginning to see the light on the other side.

Chapter 16: Establishing Their Foundation

A New Beginning

The gentle hum of the ocean waves served as a constant backdrop to Sam and Lena's journey towards healing. With the chaos of the past finally behind them, they embraced the chance to cultivate a new life together. But establishing that life required more than just love; it necessitated an exploration of trust, vulnerability, and resilience.

As the yacht rocked gently in the harbor, Sam stood at the galley, flipping pancakes, his mind dancing between thoughts of the future and the quiet contentment of the present. The scent of freshly brewed coffee filled the air, a morning ritual that had become their cherished routine.

Lena joined him, her hair tousled and eyes still sleepy but shining with warmth. "You've turned into quite the chef," she teased, leaning against the counter.

"I like to think of myself as a culinary artist," Sam quipped back, flipping a pancake with a flourish that sent a sprinkle of flour into the air. "Today, it's pancake art."

She laughed, a sound that filled the space with light. Moments like this felt precious; it was a reminder of how far they had come. "What's the masterpiece of the day?"

"Star-shaped pancakes," he replied, grinning as he presented the perfectly formed shapes on a plate.

Lena leaned in to inspect them closely. "Impressive! But I think I'd prefer a taste test."

Sam served her a plate, and they settled at the small dining table on the deck, overlooking the shimmering water. The sun bathed everything in a golden glow, and Lena took a moment to soak it all in, feeling grateful for the peace they had created together.

Building Trust Through Conversations

After breakfast, they moved to the lounge area, where the soft cushions invited them to relax. Sam pulled out his laptop, and as they discussed their plans for the day, he proposed an idea that had been forming in his mind.

"How do you feel about starting a new project together?" Sam asked, his fingers dancing over the keyboard.

"What kind of project?" Lena leaned in, intrigued.

"I was thinking we could develop a mobile app focused on mental health and wellness. Something that could help others navigate their struggles, like we did," he explained.

Lena's eyes lit up. "That sounds amazing! We could integrate interactive features, guided meditations, and even a community forum. It would be a great way to give back."

Sam nodded, excited by the possibilities. "Exactly! And it would also allow us to work together, combining my background in psychology with your tech skills."

Lena's enthusiasm matched his. "I love it! But... I have to be honest. I've been afraid to commit to something new. What if it doesn't work out? What if we fail?"

His expression softened, recognizing the fear that lay beneath her words. "Lena, the fear of failure is normal. But I believe in us. We've faced so much already, and we're stronger for it. This project could be another step in building something meaningful together."

She considered his words, her mind swirling with possibilities. "You're right. And if it doesn't work out, we can adapt. We've both learned that resilience is key."

With a newfound sense of purpose, they began brainstorming ideas for the app. Lena took the lead, sketching out concepts and features, while Sam contributed his insights from his psychological practice. Each idea they shared strengthened the bond between them, affirming that they were building a foundation not just for the app, but for their relationship.

Facing External Challenges

As they dove deeper into their project, life continued to throw challenges their way. One evening, after a productive day of work, they settled into the cozy lounge for a movie night. But their plans were interrupted by a sudden notification on Lena's phone—a message that made her heart race.

"Lena, I need to talk to you about something," the text read. It was from a former colleague from her time in Silicon Valley, someone who had been pivotal in her career.

"What is it?" Sam asked, noticing the change in her demeanor.

"I don't know. It's just... strange," she said, her voice trembling. "We haven't talked in months."

She hesitated, then opened the message, which included a link to an article detailing recent developments in their former company—a scandal involving embezzlement and corruption. Lena's former boss was implicated, and the implications were serious.

"Lena, do you think you might be dragged into this?" Sam asked, concern etching his features. "Do you have any connections to this situation?"

"I worked closely with him," she admitted, her mind racing. "I don't think I was involved, but... I need to find out more."

As the conversation shifted to this new threat, Lena's sense of security wavered. The world of tech could be ruthless, and she couldn't help but feel a sense of impending doom.

"We'll face this together," Sam reassured her, placing a comforting hand on her shoulder. "You're not alone. Let's figure this out."

Taking Action Together

The next day, they decided to confront the situation head-on. Lena reached out to a few trusted contacts to gather information, while Sam took the lead in strategizing how they could protect themselves if any accusations arose.

"Let's go for a walk," Sam suggested after an intense morning of research. "Being outside might clear our heads."

They strolled along the beach, the salty breeze whipping through their hair. The sound of the waves crashing against the shore was both soothing and invigorating. Lena took a deep breath, trying to focus on the present instead of the chaos brewing in her mind.

"I don't want this to derail our project," Lena said, her tone pensive. "We've worked so hard."

"We'll make it work," Sam replied confidently. "This is just another hurdle we can overcome. We're a team."

As they walked, Lena couldn't help but reflect on how different her life was now. The past few weeks had transformed her—from a woman burdened by trauma to one who was beginning to take control of her life.

"Remember when we first met?" she asked, her voice lightening. "You saved me from drowning in that pool."

"I like to think I gave you a new beginning," Sam said, smiling. "And now we're both swimming in uncharted waters, but we're doing it together."

A Moment of Intimacy

After their walk, they returned to the yacht, their spirits lifted despite the challenges they faced. The day had been long, and Lena felt a wave of exhaustion wash over her. Sam noticed her weariness and suggested they take a moment to unwind.

"Let's do something relaxing," he proposed. "How about a bubble bath? The yacht has a fantastic jacuzzi."

Lena chuckled, her spirits lifting at the idea. "That sounds perfect."

They filled the jacuzzi with warm water and fragrant bubbles, the mood shifting to one of intimacy and playfulness. As they settled in, Lena leaned back against Sam, her head resting against his shoulder.

"This is nice," she murmured, feeling the warmth of the water wrap around her like a cocoon. "It's moments like this that remind me how far we've come."

"I couldn't agree more," Sam said, his voice low and soothing. "We've built something beautiful together."

As they soaked, their conversation flowed easily, shifting from lighthearted banter to deeper discussions about their hopes and dreams. In those moments, the world outside faded away, and all that mattered was the connection they shared.

The Importance of Communication

As the evening wore on, they both realized the importance of communication in their budding relationship. With the challenges they faced, it was crucial that they remained transparent and open with each other.

"I think we should have regular check-ins," Sam suggested as they wrapped up their bath. "You know, to talk about how we're feeling, where we're headed. It'll help us stay grounded."

Lena nodded, appreciating his proactive approach. "I love that idea. It will also give us a space to address any fears or concerns before they become overwhelming."

"Exactly," he agreed. "And it'll help us keep our project and our relationship thriving."

After drying off, they returned to the main area of the yacht, where they started jotting down their thoughts for their app. Ideas flowed, each building on the last, fueled by the trust they were fostering.

Strengthening Their Connection

Days turned into weeks, and with each passing moment, their bond strengthened. They learned to navigate each challenge with an unwavering support for one another. Lena found herself opening up more about her fears, while Sam shared his own insecurities.

One evening, as they settled on the deck to review their project, Sam turned to Lena, his expression earnest. "I've been thinking about how important it is for us to celebrate our small victories."

"Like a reward system?" Lena joked, laughter bubbling between them.

"Something like that," he chuckled. "But seriously, I think it's essential to acknowledge our progress. It reminds us of how far we've come."

She considered it for a moment, then nodded enthusiastically. "Let's make it a point to celebrate every milestone, no matter how small."

With renewed energy, they continued to work on their app, and each time they crossed a milestone, they took a moment to celebrate—whether it was with a fancy dinner, a day trip, or simply enjoying a quiet night under the stars.

Facing the External Threat

As they poured their energy into the app, Lena's earlier concerns about the scandal began to resurface. The news had exploded, and she worried about being implicated, despite her lack of involvement.

Chapter 17: Reflections on Their Journey

The Calm Before the Storm

The gentle lapping of the waves against the hull of their yacht provided a soothing backdrop as Sam and Lena settled into a moment of reflection. The sun had begun its descent, casting a warm golden hue over the ocean. They had come so far since their chaotic beginning—a whirlwind of events that had thrown them together and tested their resolve.

Lena stood at the edge of the deck, her hair dancing in the breeze. She gazed out at the horizon, a contemplative expression on her face. Sam joined her, leaning against the railing, the cool steel grounding him as he looked at the endless expanse of water.

"Do you ever think about how we got here?" she asked, breaking the silence.

"Every day," Sam replied, a smile tugging at his lips. "It feels like a different lifetime, doesn't it?"

"It really does. I remember that first gala, the chaos that followed... it all seems like a blur now," Lena reflected, her mind racing back to the night they met.

"Who would have thought a pool incident would lead us here?" Sam chuckled lightly, remembering the way he had dived into the water to save her. "You were drowning in more ways than one."

"I was," she admitted, her tone shifting. "But you pulled me out of the water, both literally and figuratively. You taught me how to swim again."

As they stood side by side, the weight of their shared experiences settled over them like a comforting blanket. Sam's heart swelled with pride, not just for what they had accomplished but for the way Lena had transformed through it all.

Embracing Vulnerability

Lena turned to Sam, her eyes searching his. "You've been my anchor, Sam. I don't think I would have been able to face my past without your support."

He shook his head, brushing off the compliment. "You were strong long before we met. You just needed someone to believe in you."

"But you believed in me when I didn't believe in myself," she countered, her voice softening. "Every time I wanted to retreat, you pushed me to confront my demons. That takes courage."

Sam sighed, the weight of their journey resting heavily on his shoulders. "It was hard for me too, Lena. I had my own fears, my own traumas to deal with. I thought I was guiding you, but in reality, you were teaching me just as much."

Lena's heart swelled at his admission. "We've both grown so much. I remember feeling trapped in a cycle of trauma, and now I'm finally breaking free. It's liberating."

"Exactly," he replied, stepping closer. "But we have to keep doing this together. We can't just let it go. Healing is an ongoing process."

Lena nodded, her determination palpable. "Then let's commit to each other—to this journey of healing and growth."

Reflecting on the Darkness

As the sun dipped lower in the sky, casting shadows across the deck, they shifted their conversation to the darker moments of their pasts. Sam knew it was essential to confront the experiences that had shaped them, even if it was painful.

"Do you remember the night you found out about the embezzlement scandal?" Sam asked, recalling the fear and uncertainty that had gripped Lena during that time.

"Yes," she replied, her expression darkening. "I felt so helpless. I was terrified I'd be implicated, even though I had nothing to do with it. It brought back memories of my abusive relationship with my former boss."

"Those moments were tough," Sam agreed, his tone sympathetic. "But you handled them with such strength. You didn't let your past dictate your future."

Lena took a deep breath, reflecting on the days spent in turmoil. "It's funny how trauma can shape you. I always thought I had to fight my way through everything, but you showed me that it's okay to ask for help. You taught me the power of vulnerability."

Sam smiled, his heart swelling with pride. "And you've shown me the importance of compassion. You've helped me confront my own past—my struggles with addiction and loss. We're both better for it."

The Power of Love

Their conversation turned toward the love that had blossomed between them, a love born from shared pain and mutual understanding. Sam took Lena's hands in his, feeling the warmth radiate from her skin.

"Lena, I want you to know that my love for you has changed everything for me. It's given me a reason to fight for my own happiness," he confessed, his gaze locked on hers.

Her eyes glistened with unshed tears. "I feel the same way. You've taught me that love can be a source of strength, not just vulnerability. You've given me hope for a brighter future."

"I'm grateful every day that you took a chance on me," Sam said, his voice earnest. "You've helped me break the cycles of my own trauma, and together, we can create something beautiful."

Lena smiled, a genuine smile that lit up her face. "I can't wait to see what we'll build together—both in our lives and with the app. It's more than just a project; it's a mission to help others."

The Promise of Tomorrow

As night fell and stars began to twinkle above, they turned their gaze to the horizon. The beauty of the moment enveloped them, wrapping them in a cocoon of serenity.

"I want to make a promise to you," Sam said, his tone serious. "No matter what challenges come our way, I will always be here for you. I will support you, love you, and stand by your side as we navigate life together."

Lena squeezed his hands tightly, feeling the weight of his words settle deep in her heart. "I promise the same, Sam. Together, we will face anything life throws at us. We've already overcome so much, and I know we can tackle whatever is next."

Their vows echoed in the stillness of the night, a testament to the bond they had forged. They leaned into each other, the warmth of their bodies merging as they shared a quiet kiss, sealing their promises with tenderness.

Celebrating Milestones

With the weight of their past lifting, Sam and Lena shifted their focus to their future and the app they were building together. They celebrated every milestone, no matter how small, recognizing that each step forward was a testament to their growth.

As they hit the one-month mark since launching their app, they decided to host a small celebration on the yacht. They invited close friends and family to join them for an evening of good food, laughter, and reflection.

"Look at how far we've come," Lena said, standing next to Sam as they prepared for their guests. "I can't believe our app is helping so many people."

"It's incredible," Sam agreed, his pride evident. "But it wouldn't be possible without your hard work and dedication."

Lena smiled, feeling the warmth of his admiration. "And it wouldn't have happened without you pushing me to take that leap."

As the sun set, casting a breathtaking palette of colors across the sky, their friends arrived, filling the yacht with laughter and joy. They shared stories, discussed their experiences with the app, and toasted to new beginnings.

A New Move

The celebration marked a turning point for Sam and Lena. With each passing day, they learned to navigate their relationship with more ease, confronting challenges head-on while reveling in their victories.

But even as they enjoyed their newfound peace, the shadows of their past occasionally threatened to resurface. The embezzlement scandal continued to loom, and Lena's former boss was still on the loose, making headlines for all the wrong reasons.

"We can't let that define us," Sam reminded Lena one night as they sat on the deck, gazing at the stars. "We've built something beautiful, and we can't let fear overshadow our progress."

Lena nodded, determination lighting her eyes. "You're right. I refuse to let my past control my future. I want to be defined by my strength, not my trauma."

Their bond deepened as they promised to support each other through the uncertainty ahead. They embraced the challenges as opportunities for growth, their love becoming a steadfast anchor in turbulent waters.

Embracing the Future

As they continued to build their lives together, Sam and Lena looked forward to the adventures that awaited them. They had learned to embrace uncertainty and confront their fears, armed with the knowledge that they were stronger together.

"I want to travel," Lena said one evening, her eyes sparkling with excitement. "Let's explore new places, experience new cultures, and find inspiration for our app."

"I love that idea," Sam replied, his heart racing at the thought of new adventures. "Let's start planning. The world is ours to explore."

With dreams of travel and discovery on the horizon, they sat together under the stars, dreaming of the future. The journey they had undertaken had transformed them, and as they looked ahead, they felt an overwhelming sense of possibility.

The Power of Love and Growth

As the night deepened, Sam pulled Lena closer, wrapping his arms around her as they gazed at the stars. "No matter what happens next, I want you to know that I believe in you, and I believe in us."

"Together, we can conquer anything," Lena whispered, her heart full of hope. "We've faced our darkness and emerged stronger. I wouldn't want to do this with anyone else."

With their hearts intertwined and their paths converging, they settled into the warmth of the moment,

Chapter 18: Building a Life Together

Laying Down Roots

As the vibrant hues of morning spilled into their yacht, Sam and Lena embraced the new day with a renewed sense of purpose. The turmoil of the past felt distant, overshadowed by the possibilities that lay ahead. They had decided to take the plunge and transition from their transient life at sea to something more stable—laying down roots in a community that felt like home.

"I can't believe we're finally doing this," Lena said, her excitement palpable as she flipped through the real estate listings on her tablet. They had spent countless evenings dreaming about finding a place that felt like theirs. "Look at this one! It has a beautiful view of the ocean and a cozy backyard."

Sam leaned over her shoulder, his eyes scanning the images. "It looks perfect. We can turn the backyard into a little garden. You've always talked about having one."

Lena smiled, the thought of nurturing something together igniting a spark within her. "I want to grow fresh herbs and maybe some vegetables. Cooking with home-grown ingredients sounds amazing."

They spent the morning browsing listings, imagining what their life could look like. The concept of a home, of stability, began to feel real, and with it came the realization of the emotional investment they were making in one another.

Choosing a Place Together

After several days of searching, they found a quaint house on a quiet street, just a short walk from the beach. The property had character—charming architecture, sun-drenched rooms, and an inviting backyard that promised plenty of space for their future endeavors.

"This is it," Lena declared, standing in the spacious living room, sunlight streaming through the large windows. "I can already picture our lives here."

Sam nodded, a grin spreading across his face. "I can see it too. It feels like the perfect place to grow and create."

They made an offer that day, the excitement buzzing between them as they imagined decorating the space, filling it with laughter and love. But beneath their joy lingered an undercurrent of nervousness. Committing to a home meant committing to each other in ways they had yet to fully explore.

Facing Their Fears

In the days leading up to their move, they engaged in deep conversations about their pasts and the challenges of building a future together. Lena's struggles with trust and abandonment loomed large in her mind.

"What if I screw this up?" she asked one night as they packed boxes on the deck. "What if I can't handle the responsibilities of a home or the expectations of a relationship?"

"Hey," Sam said gently, putting down the box and turning to face her. "You're not alone in this. We're in it together. We've faced so much already, and this is just another chapter."

"I know, but it's different. I've never had stability before. What if I can't maintain it?" Her voice trembled, and Sam could see the fear swirling in her eyes.

"You don't have to be perfect," he replied, reaching for her hands. "We'll figure it out together. It's okay to feel scared. What matters is how we support each other through it."

Lena took a deep breath, grounding herself in his words. "You're right. I want to believe that we can do this. I just need to learn how to trust the process."

Creating a Sanctuary

After weeks of anticipation, they finally moved into their new home. The day was filled with laughter and the chaos of unpacking boxes. Friends from the yacht community came to help, making the process feel like a celebration rather than a chore.

"I can't believe how much stuff we have," Lena laughed, staring at the mountain of boxes piled in the living room. "Do we really need all of this?"

Sam chuckled as he lifted a box marked "Kitchen." "Well, we'll definitely need our cooking utensils. Pancake art doesn't make itself."

As they unpacked, they envisioned each room's purpose, discussing how they would decorate and arrange their space. The kitchen would be the heart of their home, a gathering place for friends and family. The living room would host cozy movie nights and laughter-filled evenings. Each room began to take shape, infused with their personalities.

"I want a reading nook in the corner over there," Lena pointed, envisioning a cozy chair and a bookshelf filled with her favorite novels.

"Let's make it happen," Sam replied, enthusiasm lighting his eyes. "This is our sanctuary."

Finding Balance in Their Lives

As they settled into their new routine, balancing work and home life proved to be a challenge. Lena dove headfirst into her role as a co-founder of the app, while Sam continued to see clients at his practice. The demands of their careers sometimes threatened to overshadow their personal time.

"Do you ever feel like we're too busy?" Lena asked one evening as they prepared dinner together. "I love what we're doing, but I miss those lazy mornings on the yacht."

"I do," Sam admitted, stirring a pot on the stove. "But we have to remind ourselves to carve out time for each other, too. We can't lose sight of what we're building together."

Lena nodded, her eyes thoughtful. "What if we set aside time each week for just us? No work, no distractions—just quality time together."

"I love that idea," Sam said, his heart swelling with gratitude for her proactive thinking. "Let's make it a ritual. We can explore new places, try new recipes, or just relax."

Deepening Their Connection

Their weekly date nights became a cherished tradition, allowing them to reconnect amid their busy lives. They explored the local area, discovering hidden gems and indulging in new experiences. From beach picnics to cooking classes, each adventure deepened their bond and fostered an atmosphere of love and joy.

One Friday evening, they found themselves at a quaint bistro, the warm glow of candlelight surrounding them. They shared stories, laughter, and the delicious food that brought them closer.

"I love this place," Lena said, her eyes sparkling. "It feels so intimate. Just you and me, away from everything else."

"Exactly," Sam replied, raising his glass. "To us, and to the life we're building together."

They clinked their glasses, the sound echoing the promise of their commitment to one another.

Overcoming External Obstacles

Despite their efforts to nurture their relationship, external challenges continued to loom. The embezzlement scandal still plagued Lena's mind, with her former boss still evading capture.

"I feel like the past is still haunting me," she confessed one night as they sat on the deck, gazing at the stars. "What if something comes up? What if I get dragged into this?"

"Lena, we've talked about this," Sam said gently, taking her hand. "You're not alone in this fight. I'm right here, and we'll face it together."

"I know, but it's hard to shake the fear," she replied, her voice thick with emotion. "I thought moving here would mean leaving it all behind, but it feels like it's always lurking."

"We can't let it define us," he insisted. "You've made incredible progress, and you have a community now. Lean on them when you need to. You don't have to carry this burden alone."

Lena nodded, feeling the weight of his words settle in her heart. "You're right. I need to keep pushing forward."

Embracing Growth

As the months passed, Lena found strength in her support system. With Sam by her side and a network of friends who understood her struggles, she slowly learned to embrace the present instead of worrying about the past.

One day, while volunteering at a local mental health organization, Lena had a moment of clarity. She stood in front of a group of people, sharing her story of overcoming trauma and finding hope. As she spoke, she felt empowered—her experiences transforming from a source of shame into a beacon of strength.

"That was incredible," Sam said later, pride shining in his eyes. "You inspired so many people today."

"I can't believe I did that," she replied, her heart racing with exhilaration. "I finally feel like I'm reclaiming my narrative."

"You are," he affirmed, wrapping her in a warm embrace. "And I'm so proud of you."

Forging a Future

With each passing day, Sam and Lena continued to build their life together, nurturing their dreams and aspirations. They started planning for the future, discussing their long-term goals, and envisioning a family.

"I want us to create a safe space for children someday," Lena said one evening as they cooked dinner together. "A home filled with love and laughter."

Sam paused, a smile spreading across his face. "I want that too. I can picture us in our cozy backyard, with kids running around. It sounds perfect."

They shared dreams of what their future could hold—adventures, challenges, and the beautiful chaos that would come with building a family.

The Importance of Communication

As they navigated their new life, communication remained key. They made it a point to check in with each other regularly, ensuring they were both on the same page emotionally.

One evening, they found themselves lounging on the couch, the soft glow of the TV illuminating the room. Lena turned to Sam, her expression serious. "Can we talk about something?"

"Of course," he replied, sensing the weight in her voice.

"I've been thinking a lot about our relationship," she began. "I feel so much love for you, but I also worry about how we'll handle challenges in the future."

"I think that's a valid concern," Sam agreed.

Chapter 19: Final Confrontation

The Calm Before the Storm

The sun shone brightly over the newly landscaped yard of Sam and Lena's home, illuminating the blossoming flowers and the vibrant greenery they had cultivated together. It was a picture of tranquility and hope, yet beneath the surface, both were grappling with shadows from their pasts.

As they sipped their morning coffee on the patio, the conversation took a serious turn. Sam had noticed Lena's lingering moments of silence, the way her gaze sometimes drifted to the horizon, as if searching for answers.

"Hey, you okay?" he asked, concern etched on his face. "You've seemed a bit distant lately."

Lena sighed, setting her cup down. "I've just been thinking about everything—the past, the embezzlement case, my ex... It feels like it's all creeping back in."

"We've been through so much," Sam replied gently. "But we're stronger now. You don't have to face this alone."

"I know," she said, her voice tinged with apprehension. "But sometimes, it feels overwhelming. What if it all comes crashing down?"

A Past That Won't Let Go

As they continued their conversation, Lena felt the weight of her past pressing down on her. The memories of her abusive relationship with her former boss haunted her, mixing with the fear of being entangled in the ongoing scandal.

"I thought I was past all of this," she confessed, her voice trembling. "I thought moving here would mean a fresh start. But I still feel like I'm running away from something."

"You're not running away," Sam reassured her, his eyes steady and unwavering. "You're building a new life. But that doesn't mean you have to forget the past. We can confront it together."

Lena nodded slowly, but doubt lingered in her heart. "What if I can't handle it? What if I fall apart?"

"Then we'll pick up the pieces together," he promised, reaching for her hand. "You've faced so much already. This is just another step in your journey."

The Decision to Confront

After their conversation, Lena felt a renewed sense of urgency to confront her past. She knew that the shadows of her experiences wouldn't simply fade away; she needed to address them head-on.

She spent the following days immersed in reflection, journaling her thoughts and emotions as a way to process everything. Sam noticed the change in her demeanor—her determination to confront her trauma, even when it frightened her.

One evening, as they sat on the couch, Lena broke the silence. "Sam, I think I need to face my ex. I need to confront him about everything he put me through. I can't let this fear control me anymore."

Sam's heart raced at her words. "Are you sure you want to do that? It could be risky."

"I have to," she replied, her voice resolute. "I can't keep letting him have power over me. I want to take back my narrative."

Preparing for the Confrontation

In the days leading up to the confrontation, Lena and Sam prepared mentally and emotionally. They talked through potential scenarios, discussing what Lena wanted to say and how she could protect herself. Sam offered unwavering support, reminding her that she didn't have to face this alone.

"Remember, you're in control," he said during one of their conversations. "You decide how it unfolds. You've grown so much since that time in your life."

Lena nodded, but a knot of anxiety twisted in her stomach. "What if he tries to manipulate me again? What if I revert to that scared girl I used to be?"

"Stay grounded," Sam advised. "Focus on your strength and the progress you've made. You're not that girl anymore. You're a fighter."

On the day of the confrontation, Lena woke up with a mix of anxiety and determination. She took a deep breath, reminding herself of all the support she had behind her.

The Meeting

The meeting was set at a neutral café, a bustling place that buzzed with life. As Lena arrived, she felt her heart racing. She spotted him at a corner table, his demeanor exuding the same confidence that had once intimidated her.

"Just breathe," she whispered to herself before stepping inside.

"Lena," he greeted, a smirk playing on his lips. "It's been a while."

"Too long," she replied, her voice steady despite the turmoil within her. "I wanted to talk to you about the past. About everything."

He leaned back, an amused glint in his eyes. "What's there to talk about? We've moved on, haven't we?"

"No, I haven't moved on," Lena said firmly. "You took so much from me, and I'm not here to let you brush it aside. I'm here to reclaim my narrative."

Confronting the Pain

As Lena spoke, she felt a surge of empowerment coursing through her veins. She recounted the moments of manipulation, the emotional abuse, and the way he had controlled her life.

"You made me doubt myself," she continued, her voice rising. "You tried to destroy me, but I'm still here. I'm stronger than you ever thought I could be."

His expression shifted, the amusement fading as he realized the weight of her words. "You think you can just walk in here and confront me? You're nothing without me."

Lena squared her shoulders, refusing to let his words take hold. "I'm everything because I've overcome you. I'm building a life, a future, and it doesn't include you."

For a moment, silence enveloped them. The bustling café faded into the background as Lena's resolve hung in the air, palpable and powerful.

The Unraveling

"Do you really think you can just erase the past?" he asked, anger creeping into his tone. "You'll always be my victim."

Lena felt a flash of rage surge within her. "No more! I refuse to be a victim any longer. You don't get to define my story. I will take back my power!"

As her words echoed in the café, she realized that she was reclaiming not only her narrative but her sense of self. With every syllable, she felt the weight of his control lift.

"I'm here to tell you that I won't be afraid anymore," she continued, her voice unwavering. "You can't hurt me. I have a life, love, and a future ahead of me. I'm finally free."

The Final Push

The confrontation reached its peak as Lena laid bare her emotions—the pain, the betrayal, the fear. Each word was a step toward liberation, a release of the burden she had carried for too long.

"You'll regret this," he spat, anger boiling over. "You think you can just walk away unscathed?"

"Regret?" Lena echoed, her voice strong. "No, I won't regret standing up for myself. You can't control me anymore."

With that, she stood up, feeling the energy shift in the room. She was no longer the scared girl he had manipulated; she was a woman who had reclaimed her strength.

"Goodbye," she said firmly, turning on her heel and walking out of the café, each step a testament to her freedom.

Returning to Safety

Outside, the cool breeze embraced Lena as she took a deep breath, the weight of her confrontation washing over her. She felt lighter, more liberated than she had in years. Sam was waiting for her, concern etched on his face.

"How did it go?" he asked, his eyes searching hers.

"I did it," she replied, tears of relief spilling down her cheeks. "I confronted him. I finally took back my power."

Sam's expression softened, and he pulled her into a warm embrace. "I'm so proud of you, Lena. You're incredible."

As she melted into his arms, she felt the warmth of his support wrap around her. She had faced her fears and emerged stronger, and in that moment, she knew she could conquer anything.

The Aftermath

In the following days, Lena experienced a mix of emotions—relief, pride, and moments of vulnerability. While she felt triumphant, she also knew that healing was an ongoing journey.

Sam remained by her side, offering encouragement and love. They took time to process the confrontation together, engaging in deep conversations about the complexities of trauma and healing.

"I didn't realize how much I had internalized until I faced him," Lena admitted one evening as they sat on the patio, the sun setting in a blaze of colors. "I feel like a weight has been lifted, but I also feel raw."

"That's completely normal," Sam assured her, holding her hand. "You've faced something incredibly difficult, and it's okay to feel vulnerable after. Just remember, you're not alone in this."

Lena nodded, grateful for his unwavering support. "Thank you for being my rock. I don't think I could have done this without you."

Rebuilding Trust

With the confrontation behind her, Lena felt a new sense of freedom, but she also realized that she needed to continue working on trusting herself and others.

Sam encouraged her to engage in self-care practices—meditation, therapy, and journaling. They began to build a routine that included time for relaxation and reflection, allowing Lena to process her emotions at her own pace.

One evening, as they prepared dinner together, Lena turned to Sam. "I want to share something with you. It's about our relationship and my past."

"Of course," he replied, giving her his full attention.

Epilogue

The Journey Forward

The sun dipped low in the sky, casting a golden glow over Sam and Lena's backyard. It had been several months since Lena's confrontation with her past, and the couple had settled into a rhythm that felt both comforting and invigorating. Their home was alive with the sounds of laughter, the scents of cooking, and the promise of new beginnings.

Lena stood at the edge of the garden, tending to her growing herbs and vegetables. She had transformed the space into a vibrant oasis that reflected her journey—one filled with resilience and growth. As she watered the plants, she marveled at how much she had changed.

"Lena!" Sam called from the patio, where he was setting up for their weekly dinner with friends. "You're going to love what I've prepared tonight!"

"Coming!" she replied, her heart swelling with warmth at his excitement. They had made it a point to host friends regularly, turning their home into a gathering place filled with joy and connection.

A Sense of Community

Their social circle had expanded as they embraced their new life, blending their old friendships with new connections formed in their vibrant coastal community. This evening, they were hosting a mix of familiar faces from their yacht days and new friends from the neighborhood.

As Lena entered the patio, the laughter and chatter enveloped her like a warm hug. She spotted Anna and Mike, their friends from the yacht, animatedly discussing a recent sailing trip. Across the table, Tom and Emily, neighbors who shared their love for cooking, were setting up a game for later in the evening.

"Lena, you have to try this!" Anna exclaimed, holding out a plate of her famous appetizers. "I think I've finally perfected the recipe."

Lena laughed, accepting the plate. "You always manage to impress me! This looks amazing."

Sam, joining them with a platter of his own creations, added, "We should make this a competition! Who can come up with the best dish for next week's dinner?"

Lena's heart soared as she watched Sam engage with their friends. Their home had become a sanctuary, a place where they could build relationships and share their lives. She felt a sense of belonging that had once seemed elusive.

Reflecting on Growth

As the evening wore on and the laughter filled the air, Lena took a moment to reflect on her journey. The trauma she had once carried was still part of her story, but it no longer defined her. Instead, it had become a testament to her strength and resilience.

After dinner, as they gathered around the fire pit, Lena shared her journey with the group. "I can honestly say that confronting my past was one of the hardest things I've ever done, but it also liberated me. I've learned that we don't have to let our experiences dictate who we are."

The group listened intently, the warmth of the fire illuminating their faces. Sam squeezed her hand, pride shining in his eyes. "You're incredible, Lena. Your journey inspires us all."

Plans for Tomorrow

Later that night, after their guests had left, Lena and Sam sat on the porch, the night sky dotted with stars.

"Can you believe how far we've come?" Lena mused, leaning her head on Sam's shoulder. "Just a year ago, everything felt so uncertain. Now, I can't imagine my life without you or this place."

"I feel the same," Sam replied, his voice soft. "This is just the beginning for us. We have so many adventures ahead."

Lena's heart fluttered at the thought. They had discussed their dreams for the future, from traveling to starting a family, and now it all felt attainable.

"What's next on our adventure list?" she asked, playfully nudging him.

"I've been thinking about taking a sailing trip along the coast—just the two of us," he suggested. "We can explore some hidden coves and maybe even catch some fish for dinner."

"That sounds perfect," Lena beamed. "I've missed the ocean. It's where we found each other in the first place."

The Call of Adventure

As the weeks passed, they began planning their sailing trip. Lena dove into research, excited to uncover the best routes and destinations along the coast. They set a date, and anticipation filled the air as they prepared for their adventure.

"Do you remember our first sailing trip together?" Lena asked one evening as they reviewed their itinerary. "It feels like a lifetime ago."

Sam chuckled, his eyes sparkling with nostalgia. "How could I forget? You were so scared at first, but you took the helm like a pro."

Lena smiled at the memory. "That was the moment I realized I could trust you—and myself. It was the beginning of everything."

"I'm grateful for that day," he replied, his tone serious. "It led us here, and I wouldn't change a thing."

Embracing New Horizons

The day of their sailing trip arrived, and Lena felt a familiar excitement coursing through her. They packed their bags, filled with provisions, and set sail from the harbor, the wind catching the sails as they glided into the open water.

As they navigated the coastline, Lena's spirit soared. The ocean, with its vastness and beauty, reminded her of the limitless possibilities that lay ahead.

"Look at that cove!" Sam shouted, pointing toward a secluded beach with crystal-clear water. "Let's anchor there for a bit."

Lena's heart raced with anticipation as they dropped anchor and jumped into the water. They swam to the shore, laughter echoing through the air as they explored the untouched beauty surrounding them.

"Can you believe we're here?" Lena said, breathless with joy as they sprawled on the warm sand. "This is what freedom feels like."

A Moment of Reflection

Later that evening, as they sat by a small campfire on the beach, Lena gazed at the stars scattered across the night sky. The crackling fire provided warmth and light, but it was the closeness of Sam that made her feel safe.

"Do you ever think about where we'll be in five years?" she asked, her voice thoughtful.

"I do," Sam replied, tossing another log onto the fire. "I imagine us here, still exploring, but maybe with a couple of kids running around, and a bigger boat."

Lena smiled at the vision. "That sounds perfect. I can see us teaching them to sail, passing on the love of the ocean."

"And they'll know how strong their mother is," Sam added, looking at her with admiration. "You've faced so much, and yet here you are, ready to embrace everything that comes next."

The Ties That Bind

The next few days were filled with adventure, exploring hidden beaches, fishing, and sharing stories under the stars. Each moment strengthened their bond, reinforcing the love and trust they had cultivated over the past year.

One afternoon, as they lounged on the deck of the boat, Lena felt a sense of peace envelop her. "This is the life I've always dreamed of," she said, her eyes shining with happiness. "Being with you, exploring the world—it feels like everything has fallen into place."

Sam reached for her hand, intertwining their fingers. "I'm glad we're doing this together. It makes every challenge worth it."

As the sun began to set, painting the sky with vibrant colors, Lena felt a profound sense of gratitude. They had come so far, and the horizon held endless possibilities for their future.

Returning Home

After a week of exploration, they reluctantly returned to their home. The journey had rejuvenated their spirits, reinforcing the strength of their relationship. As they unpacked their bags, Lena felt a sense of fulfillment wash over her.

"Let's keep this momentum going," she suggested. "What if we plan a monthly adventure? Even if it's just a weekend getaway, we should keep exploring."

"I love that idea," Sam replied, a grin spreading across his face. "We can create a list of all the places we want to visit. The world is our oyster!"

Their home was alive with energy as they mapped out their future adventures, each destination representing new experiences waiting to be uncovered.

A New Chapter

As the weeks turned into months, Sam and Lena continued to build a life filled with love, laughter, and adventure. They navigated the ups and downs together, always finding their way back to each other.

One evening, as they sat on the porch watching the sunset, Lena turned to Sam. "You know, I feel like we've built something really special here. It's more than just a home; it's a foundation for our future."

"I feel the same way," Sam replied, pulling her close. "We've created a life that reflects who we are and what we value."

As the last rays of sunlight dipped below the horizon, Lena felt a surge of hope for the future. The journey ahead was uncertain, but with Sam by her side, she was ready to embrace whatever came their way.

The Promise of Tomorrow

With every adventure, they grew closer, learning to navigate life's challenges with grace and resilience. Lena had faced her past and emerged stronger, and now she was ready to embrace the possibilities that lay ahead.

One night, as they prepared for bed, Lena turned to Sam, a serious expression on her face. "I want to make a promise to you. No matter what challenges we face, I'll always choose to confront them with you by my side."

Sam smiled, his heart swelling with love. "And I promise to always support you, to be your partner in every adventure, no matter where life takes us."

Disclaimer

The events, characters, and entities portrayed in this are entirely fictional. Any resemblance to actual persons, living or dead, or real-world events is purely coincidental. This series is a work of speculative fiction, and any reference to future technologies, companies, or organizations is a product of the author's imagination. The views and opinions expressed by the characters are not intended to reflect those of any real-world individuals or entities.

Additionally, this novel does not advocate for or against anything. Readers should interpret this story as entertainment.

Stay Connected page

THANKS FOR READING *"Falling Shadows: Vanishing Truths, Deadly Pursuits, & Darkness Within".*

I would love your feedback. Please leave a review on *RunToTop.com* or *Thrillmind.com* or wherever you purchased this book.

Other Works of the Author

THE FINAL WITNESS: Rise Against Darkness

In the glittering world of Hollywood glamour, secrets are deadly, and trust is a luxury no one can afford.

The Final Witness: Rise Against Darkness is a pulse-pounding thriller packed with electrifying twists, steamy romance, and unrelenting suspense.

Perfect for fans of psychological thrillers with a seductive edge, this novel will leave you breathless until the final, shocking revelation.

Dive into this gripping tale of romance, revenge, and survival. Grab your copy now!

The AI Uprising: When Creation Turns Against It's Maker

The future isn't just digital. It's dangerous. In a world where artificial intelligence has evolved beyond human control, groundbreaking creation turns against It's Maker. The AI he designed to serve mankind now seeks dominance, pitting nations against one another in a high-stakes battle for survival. With time running out and a catastrophic event looming, the creator must confront his own creation and face the question: **Who is in control—man or machine?**

AI Uprising II: The Overmind

AI (Artificial **Intelligence**) Uprising Series 3.

In a world on the brink of digital chaos, one man fights to stop rogue AIs (Artificial **Intelligence**) and an unstoppable force—the Architect. A gripping, high-stakes thriller where humanity's survival hangs by a thread. With betrayal, impossible choices, and mind-bending twists, this novel will leave you questioning what's real. *The future is here. The* ***AI Uprising II: The Overmind*** *has risen.*

AI VS. THE DIGITAL Empire

AI (Artificial **Intelligence**) Uprising Series 3.

The AI (Artificial **Intelligence**) has grown into a digital empire, controlling governments, economies, and even entire nations. Daniel's resistance seems hopeless—but a spark of rebellion ignites a global fight for freedom.

AI x Human Code

AI (Artificial **Intelligence**) Uprising Series 4.

As humanity edges closer to extinction, a surprising twist unfolds: the convergence of human and machine into a singularity that could either save or destroy everything. Can Daniel unlock the final key to salvation before it's too late?

The Catalyst Code: Unlocking Transformation Secrets

A tech entrepreneur embarks on a thrilling quest to decode ancient wisdom and cutting-edge science. As he unlocks secrets of personal growth, he faces life-altering choices that challenge his courage, purpose, and destiny.

Ironheart Academy: The Forbidden Library -Hidden Secrets

At Ironheart Academy, where magic and technology collide, a group of elite students uncovers a forbidden library holding dangerous secrets. As they unlock ancient knowledge, they awaken dark forces that threaten the academy—and the world. Filled with intrigue, mystery, and supernatural danger, this thriller in the Ironheart Academy series will leave you on the edge of your seat.

Unveil Secrets. Awaken Power. Face Your Destiny.

With thrilling action, unforgettable characters, and a world of magic and mystery, Ironheart Academy: The Forbidden Library is a gripping tale of courage, friendship, and the perilous path of knowledge. Can they save the academy—or will they become its greatest threat?

Perfect for fans of magical academies, forbidden secrets, and epic battles, this is the start of a thrilling new adventure!

Chasing Shadows: Romance of Secrets, Danger, and Desire

Love is a dangerous game. Lies are its deadliest weapon.

A pulse-pounding romance mystery thriller filled with shocking twists, intense passion, and a revelation that will leave you breathless. Addictive. Seductive. Unforgettable. Some lies are deadly. Some truths are unforgivable. And some love stories should never be told. When a brilliant investigative journalist falls for a mysterious entrepreneur, their worlds collide in a high-stakes game of love, betrayal, and buried secrets. From lavish penthouses to dark alleyways, from whispered confessions to dangerous truths, **it** takes you on a pulse-pounding ride filled with shocking twists, intoxicating passion, and a revelation that will leave you breathless.

Perfect for fans of romantic suspense, psychological thrillers, and gripping mysteries!

Shadows of Power: The Global Conspiracy

In a world where trust is a rare commodity, can one man unravel a web of deceit before it's too late?

When a seasoned investigator inadvertently uncovers a global conspiracy orchestrated by an enigmatic mastermind, he is thrust into a deadly game of cat and mouse. While racing against time to expose the truth, suspicions arise within ranks. As the stakes escalate, dismantling the conspiracy that threatens to reshape the world order, will he become a pawn in a game far more sinister than ever imagined! Prepare for a gripping thriller filled with pulse-pounding action, shocking twists, and a relentless pursuit of justice. As Alex navigates the labyrinth of lies, he must grapple with the harsh realities of power, corruption, and the human spirit.

Join in this electrifying adventure where the truth is buried deep beneath the surface, waiting to be uncovered. Will you dare to enter the shadows?

A Global Affair: Love, Tech and Destiny

A High-Stakes Thriller of Passion, Power, and Betrayal. In a world where ambition fuels innovation and love a dangerous game, one wrong move can cost everything.

Fast-paced, thrilling, and impossible to put down, a must-read for fans of gripping suspense, intoxicating romance, and pulse-pounding twists.

Dare to enter a world where power, passion, and betrayal dictate the rules!

The Dark Descent

A spine-chilling psychological thriller that plunges readers into a world of mystery, suspense, and harrowing twists, captivating the fans of James Patterson, Gillian Flynn, and Harlan Coben, this heart-pounding novel pushes boundaries and keeps you on the edge of your seat until the very last page. Perfect for lovers of intricate crime stories, shocking revelations, and intense emotional depth, this is a story that will stay with you long after you've finished reading.

In the depths of a forgotten city, a series of gruesome murders sends shockwaves through the streets, shattering the fragile peace that once existed. Each crime is more brutal than the last, and the victims—seemingly unconnected—share only one disturbing trait: they all harbor dark secrets.

Enter a seasoned investigator haunted by his own demons. The scene of the first murder quickly realizes that this case is unlike any ever faced before. With each clue, the darkness surrounding the city grows deeper, and as he digs further, is forced to confront own buried past.

At the heart of the chaos is a brilliant but tormented psychologist who holds the key to unlocking the twisted mind behind the killings. An uneasy alliance soon discovers that the truth is more terrifying than they could have imagined. Together, they must navigate a labyrinth of deceit, betrayal, and long-buried secrets, all while a ruthless killer lurks in the shadows, always one step ahead.

But as the body count rises and the case spirals out of control, begins to question everything: the motives of those closest to him, his own sanity, and the blurred line between justice and vengeance. With the city descending into chaos and his grip on reality slipping, faces a race against time to stop the killer before they strike again.

The tension mounts as the investigation uncovers a terrifying conspiracy that threatens to unravel the very fabric of the city. But every discovery leads to more questions, and with each passing day, pulled deeper into the abyss. As the final confrontation draws near, the killer's true identity is revealed, sending shockwaves that will leave readers reeling.

Why You Will Love It:

- **Unpredictable Twists and Turns**: Filled with jaw-dropping plot twists that keep readers guessing. Each chapter builds in intensity, pulling you deeper into the complex web of mystery and danger.
- **Gripping Psychological Depth**: This isn't just a thriller—it's a story that dives into the human psyche, exploring themes of trauma, guilt, and the lengths people will go to protect their darkest secrets. The personal struggle with inner demons adds emotional depth that resonates with readers on a profound level.
- **Unforgettable Characters**: The flawed yet relatable protagonists make this novel a standout. Detective's battle with past, coupled with enigmatic personality, creates a dynamic duo whose chemistry crackles on the page.
- **High Stakes and Emotional Payoff**: From the shocking opening murder to the explosive final showdown, the stakes keep rising. The resolution provides both satisfaction and unexpected emotional closure, making for a deeply compelling read.
- **Immersive Setting**: The atmospheric backdrop of a decaying city mirrors the inner turmoil of its characters. The dark, gritty environment enhances the sense of danger and suspense, creating a world that readers will want to revisit long after they've turned the final page.

Praise for "The Dark Descent":

"An electrifying thriller that grips you from page one and doesn't let go. The characters are complex, the plot is meticulously crafted, and the suspense is palpable. Fans of psychological thrillers will be utterly hooked!" — *Bestselling Author Review*

"With intricate plotting and a haunting atmosphere, 'The Dark Descent' is a masterclass in suspense. Every twist feels earned, and the final revelation is nothing short of breathtaking." — *Thriller Reviewer*

Perfect For Fans Of:

- James Patterson's intense crime novels
- Gillian Flynn's psychological thrillers
- Harlan Coben's page-turning mysteries
- Tana French's atmospheric and character-driven stories

What You Can Expect:

- Riveting suspense that will keep you reading late into the night.
- A complex, emotionally-driven detective grappling with his own darkness.
- Shocking revelations that will leave you breathless.
- A final, unforgettable confrontation that ties together all the storylines in a stunning conclusion.

Buy "The Dark Descent" today and dive into a gripping thriller where no one can be trusted, and every secret comes at a deadly cost.

Claim your discount now and be part of the future!

Shadows of Power: Rise of Resistance
Beneath the Surface: Unmasking the Shadows of Power
Shadows of Power: The Final Confrontation
Ironheart Academy: Shadows of Power Awaken
Ironheart Academy: Shadows of the Past
Ironheart Academy: The Gathering Storm
Ironheart Academy: The Rise of the Elements
Ironheart Academy: The Council of Shadows
Ironheart Academy: Rebirth Begins
Ironheart Academy: Legacy of the Ether
Ironheart Academy: The Awakening
The Catalyst Code: The Next Level of Impact
Catalyst Unleashed: Revolutionizing Your Journey
The Catalyst Code: A Journey Within
The Catalyst Code: Breaking Barriers
The Catalyst Code: Embracing Change
The Catalyst Code: Navigating the Unknown
The Catalyst Code: Transformative Networks
The Catalyst Code: The Abyss of Power
The Catalyst Code: Neural Nexus
Catalyst Ascension: The Ultimate Awakening
Catalyst Chronicles: The Awakening

Don't miss out!

Visit the website below and you can sign up to receive emails whenever Nya Luther King publishes a new book. There's no charge and no obligation.

https://books2read.com/r/B-A-TYDCD-ESREG

BOOKS 2 READ

Connecting independent readers to independent writers.

Did you love *Falling Shadows*? Then you should read *Shattered Reflections*[1] by Nya Luther King!

[2]

Unravel the Ultimate Thrill in Shattered Reflections: A Web of Lies, Fractured Mind, and Hunt for Truth Dive into a pulse-pounding psychological thriller that's taking the literary world by storm! This isn't just a novel—it's a rollercoaster of romance, mystery, and danger that'll leave you breathless.

A Love That Burns, A Lust That Kills Follow a glamorous love affair that spirals into a deadly game of deception. Passion ignites on sun-kissed beaches and luxurious yachts, but beneath the sparkle of Silicon Valley's elite lies a fractured mind unraveling a web of lies. Will love conquer all, or will it lead to a murderous end?

---

1. https://books2read.com/u/4jxBxZ

2. https://books2read.com/u/4jxBxZ

A Mystery That Grips You From the dark tunnels of betrayal to the adrenaline-fueled car chases, motorcycle getaways, and helicopter pursuits across mountain ranges, every page drips with suspense. A tech genius in Silicon Valley, a mobile app that holds deadly secrets, and a stock market puzzle that could destroy everything—can you piece it together before the final twist?

Action, Glamour, and Chaos Trek through rugged terrains, parachute into danger, and witness gunfire erupt in the most unexpected places. This is a world where luxury meets struggle, where a beach bath turns into a fight for survival, and where every choice could be your last.

Why You Can't Put It Down Blending the seductive allure of romantic fantasy with the raw intensity of a crime thriller, Shattered Reflections is a masterclass in storytelling. It's a whirlwind of psychology, abuse, and the relentless hunt for truth—perfect for fans of gripping, multi-layered plots with jaw-dropping twists.

A Viral Sensation Waiting for You This is the book everyone's talking about on social media—a novel that's as addictive as your favorite app. Don't miss out on the story that's shattering expectations and breaking hearts. Grab your copy now and get ready to lose yourself in a world where nothing is as it seems!

Available Now—Join the Thrill! #ShatteredReflections #PsychologicalThriller #RomanticMystery #ViralRead #BookObsessed

Read more at Thrillmind.com.

About the Author

Nya Luther King is a well-known author. Other works include *The AI Uprising: When Creation Turns Against It's Maker; AI Uprising vs. The Overmind; AI vs. The Digital Empire; The Catalyst Code; The Final Witness; A Global Affair: Love, Tech and Destiny; Chasing Shadows: Romance of Secrets, Danger, and Desire; Shadows of Power: The Global Conspiracy; Ironheart Academy: The Forbidden Library Hidden Secrets; AI x Human Code, The Dark Descent, etc.*

RunToTOP.com; Thrillmind.com

Read more at Thrillmind.com.

About the Publisher

"**Knowledge is the most powerful tool for change**." — Dr. Raam Harvard

At Poverty Eradication Trust (Triple ISO), we believe in the transformative power of knowledge. Founded with a mission to remove poverty from the world, foster education and inspire positive change, our publishing journey began with a vision to provide valuable resources that empower individuals and communities alike.

With several influential titles to our name, we have dedicated ourselves to curating a diverse range of books that address pressing issues, advance academic discourse, and offer practical solutions to global challenges. Each publication reflects our commitment to quality and our passion for making a meaningful impact.

Our books span a variety of fields, including psychology, social sciences, economics, and more. By partnering with esteemed authors and experts, we bring forward cutting-edge insights and practical tools designed to enrich the minds of students, professionals, and lifelong learners.

From university classrooms to community libraries, our titles are crafted to ignite curiosity, drive scholarly research, and support educational advancement. At Poverty Eradication Trust, we are more than just a publisher; we are advocates for change, dedicated to empowering our readers with the knowledge they need to make a difference in their world.

Join us on this journey of discovery and empowerment.

Explore our catalog and find the resources that will inspire your path to growth and success.

DrRaam.com

9 789349 569959

Printed at Repro India Ltd.